Wish

by

C. Dow Moore

DORRANCE
PUBLISHING CO
EST. 1920
PITTSBURGH, PENNSYLVANIA 15233

The contents of this work, including, but not limited to, the accuracy of events, people, and places depicted; opinions expressed; permission to use previously published materials included; and any advice given or actions advocated are solely the responsibility of the author, who assumes all liability for said work and indemnifies the publisher against any claims stemming from publication of the work.

All Rights Reserved
Copyright © 2018 by C. Dow Moore

No part of this book may be reproduced or transmitted, downloaded, distributed, reverse engineered, or stored in or introduced into any information storage and retrieval system, in any form or by any means, including photocopying and recording, whether electronic or mechanical, now known or hereinafter invented without permission in writing from the publisher.

Dorrance Publishing Co
585 Alpha Drive
Pittsburgh, PA 15238
Visit our website at *www.dorrancebookstore.com*

ISBN: 978-1-4809-9159-0
eISBN: 978-1-4809-9373-0

For my son Tyler, who encouraged me to write this book and will probably never read it.

Acknowledgments

There are many people that helped me with this book, both directly and indirectly. First, I would like to thank my family who helped shape who I am and provided me with a wonderful childhood full of many great memories. To my father, Charles "Charlie" Moore, who is the best story teller I know. He was the guy that everyone wanted to sit with at the Christmas parties because there were bound to be stories and jokes the whole evening. To Mom, she gave me the love of books and reading. I can still remember going to the Stuart Library on East Ocean Blvd. and getting armfuls of books, week after week. Then, we moved onto the used book stores. Right before I graduated college, we flew to Painesville, Ohio to visit my grandparents. The local library was having a book sale, and everything was twenty-five cents. We bought so many books; we had to buy two extra suitcases to carry them all back. Both bags exceeded the fifty-pound limit. I still have books on my shelf with "Property of Painesville Library" on the spine. And to my sister, Janeen, who provided me with the best advice one could give a first-time author struggling with a story; stay true to yourself, which I did. Thanks Jeannie!

Dennis and Karen Stultz are very good friends of mine that I have known for several years. They were instrumental in helping me get the job I still have today, and that was over three years ago. And I need their intelligent conversation, although Dennis might question the use of "intelligent" regarding my input. Being a former law enforcement officer on many levels, he was crucial with helping me with the legal angles of the story. I also credit him with "N.H.I." You'll get to it. There was a point that I texted him a question regarding something, and he replied back the next day. I gave him a hard time about his punctuality, and he pointed out he was in surgery. My bad.

I have known Henry Fell for over twenty-five years. I have a handful of friends like that, and I am truly grateful for each of them. Because of his business, I get to see him twice a year on conventions. It was him that twice pulled me off the ledge when I wasn't sure if the book made any sense or not. And it was him who made me promise that I wouldn't give up. Thank you, Henry! Next time I see you, let's make a "Plan for the end of Day!"

Suzy is one of my best friends, and she helped me with all the computer related stuff. I have difficulties operating my email, and she was able to transfer my material from the living room computer to the one in the bedroom connected to the internet. And she did this several times. When she asked why I don't just write it in the bedroom, I responded with a grocery list of reasons why I prefer the living room. She's known me a long time and thankfully has accepted most of my quirks and flaws. At the beginning, she informed me that I needed a "flash drive." For two days, I thought it was pornography in cars; that's how clueless I am and how much I needed her help. Thank you!

Christopher Hollbrook, my good friend and my doppelganger. He is a true Floridian, like myself, who appreciates where we grew up. He helped me with the nutria information for the taco shop and many of the environmental aspects for the book. I thank you. I got the pleasure of visiting him last summer, and he asked what he could cook for me. Without hesitation, I responded with, "Blackened shrimp and bleu cheese grits;" a southern staple. He said we needed to go to the store, which in my mind meant hours getting ingredients. All he needed was butter. He had everything including the anchovy paste for the homemade Caesar salad dressing. I stirred grits for an hour while he braised the romaine with a propane blow torch. It was the best meal I ever had. Apparently, he made the same meal for his future in-laws and won them over. He and his wife live in Tallahassee, Florida.

Michael Joseph Finnell. What can I say? My best friend from high school that I still keep in contact with on a regular basis was an inspiration for the book. I modeled one of the characters after him, and the inside joke is law enforcement was the last thing he wanted to do in life; especially after "the great lobster release" at Stuart Fine Foods grocery store when he was 17. Many of the memories I shared in the book, he was a part of. And yes, there really was *Llama van.*

The graphic artist Lulu Lollipop designed the book cover from a drawing my son made. It is absolutely perfect. Thank you so much. I look forward to working with you on the next book, *Hope.*

Thank you, Dorrance Publishing, for all the hard work that went into the book. I want to thank everyone that helped with *Wish,* especially Shaina Ott, my Project Coordinator. She was extremely patient with me and my many phone calls. Thank you!

Make a Wish is an actual foundation that helps terminally ill children receive the resources they need for their "wish." For more information, please visit *www.wish.org.*

And finally, to my fellow classmates from Susan Spraker's Creative Writing class at the University of Central Florida in 2002. Those of you who skewered my poetry and tore apart my short stories, I thank you. I used the back side of your critiques to write the outline for *Wish* and used it for inspiration. I have one word for you. "Ha!"

I

Scott Cooper looked at himself in the mirror and sighed. *What am I doing? I'm officially the worst security guard in the world.* His white, button down shirt and blue polyester pants, with the eternal crease in the front and back, hung on his thin frame. The clip-on tie was crooked no matter how much he tried to straighten it. And he already lost his badge, so he grabbed one from his son's playsets. He hoped no one would notice it said "Galaxy Patrol." He parted his dark brown hair the same way he had since high school and applied some after shave to his cheeks. After completing two eight-hour classes and paying a 50-dollar processing fee, Scott Cooper was recognized by the State of Florida as a class one, security officer. A friend of his pulled some strings and got him a job at a resort for handicapped and terminally ill children called Granted Wishes Village. Because there was a very small probability that he would encounter any actual violence, Scott took the job. His entire life, Scott Cooper had never raised his fists in anger at anyone and avoided confrontations at all costs. *The kids are in wheelchairs. How dangerous can it be?*

The moment that came to define Scott Cooper's non-confrontational and passive attitude was in the London Underground when he was 11-years-old. His father, Charles Cooper, had business in London, England, so he decided to fly the family and his mother-in-law there with him. The 12-hour flight was grueling for Scott and his younger brother Joey, but they played cards and did puzzles until they landed. Scott could barely understand the people of England when they talked, even though they spoke the same language. While Mr. Cooper held his meetings during the day, Mrs. Cooper, Nana, Scott, and Joey would explore London. They saw Big Ben, Parliament, and the Tower of London. His mother dragged them to countless museums, and they took several tours with guides. They were headed back to the hotel to meet up with Scott's dad and had to take the English subway or the Underground. The subway car was full because it was late in the afternoon, and people were getting off of work and heading home. Nana and Mrs. Cooper held onto the pole, and Scott held his younger brother's hand. As he stood there, he looked around at the crowd gathered on the afternoon commute. There was a man standing next to him that had an overcoat draped over his hands. He had dark, greasy hair and looked as if he hadn't shaved in days. Scott watched the man and noticed that with one hand he held the coat, but the other hand was going through the purse of the woman standing next to him. He was using the overcoat as cover to pickpocket. Scott looked up at the man who looked at him, right in the eyes. He didn't smile, nor did he stop what he was doing. And Scott just froze. He didn't do anything because he didn't know what to do. Nana was having one of her dizzy spells, so his mother was busy looking after her, and it was his job to look after Joey. Scott knew that stealing was wrong, and he should do something, but instead he quickly looked at the floor. The man found a wallet and put it under his coat and turned around. When the next stop came, he quickly sprinted off the subway car, and Scott just stood there, holding his little brother's hand and feeling ashamed for not stopping the man or at least saying something. The next stop would be another defining moment in Scott's life.

Scott Cooper held many odd jobs in his career. The shortest being the one day spent as a gardener at Our Lady of Peace Cemetery. It took him nearly an hour to get up the courage to mow over the actual plots. The idea of someone dead directly underneath him gave him an uneasy feeling. He had knocked over two headstones with the massive lawn mower before turning a floral display on a grave to confetti. As the shredded lilies floated to the ground, Scott could make out the Foreman running to him, waving his arms frantically in the air, shouting something he couldn't make out over the sound of the mower. Scott Cooper could only conclude that he was coming by to politely tell him that his services were no longer required. Of course, in reality, there were a lot of four letter words mixed in. But this, this job as a security guard, was completely off the reservation for Scott Cooper. He was average weight, 165 pounds and average height: five foot nine inches. Nothing about him was imposing, intimidating, or threatening. And the fact he had a baby face and looked much younger than his age contributed. Scott had mastered the art of staying under the radar, so he was very nervous about his first day of work where his role was to be the radar. Scott drove up to the guard shack at Granted Wishes Village at 5:45 am and was greeted by the overnight security guard.

"You must be the new guy. I'm Henry Weisel," the security guard said. Scott noticed the uniform looked much better on Henry than it did himself. He was the same height as Scott and had the same thin frame, but he had long hair that hung on his head, and he had a goatee.

"Scott Cooper," Scott said and extended his hand out of the window of his car.

"Welcome to the most boring job on the planet," Henry said. *Perfect*, Scott thought as the gate went up and he drove to the Administration building. Scott parked his car and followed the sidewalk to the entrance. At the entrance to the building was a stuffed possum the size of Scott. He held a large, golden scepter in his right paw, wore a purple robe, and had a crown on his head. And he had a name badge that said, "Pete." The grey fur was matted like it had been out in the rain too much.

"Hi folks! Welcome to Granted Wishes Village. We hope you enjoy your stay here. We want your every wish to be our command," a speaker inside Pete Possum's mouth said. *Interesting,* Scott thought. To anyone not raised in the south, a possum looks like a big, fat rat with a long, hairless tail and pointy teeth. The idea that someone thought that a five-foot tall rodent would be an appropriate mascot amused Scott Cooper as he entered the building. *But then again,* he thought, *I live in Central Florida where the face of a mouse is plastered everywhere.* He passed through the lobby and approached the desk. The young woman behind the desk smiled at him. She was young and attractive but in a modest way. Her hair was pulled into a pony tail, and she wore very little makeup.

"Welcome to Granted Wishes Village. You must be our new security guard," she said with a pleasant voice. "I'll let Mr. Kawalski know you're here." She picked up the phone, and after a few seconds, she said, "He's here." A moment later, a burly man with a red crew cut and a bushy, walrus-like mustache barreled down the hall way.

"Lenny Kawalski," he said. He extended a meaty paw of a hand at Scott, and they shook hands. Just as Scott surmised by his big stature, he had a grip like a gorilla.

"Scott Cooper," Scott said. He followed Lenny back down the hallway to his office. On the walls were paintings of the Board of Directors and the founder, Lillian Stultzman. She looked like everyone's grandma. Old, wrinkled, grey hair, and a smile that warmed your heart. At the end of the hallway was Lenny's office, and Scott was greeted with a wall of University of Wisconsin sports memorabilia. A jersey with the number 71 was incased in glass on the wall. There was a football with a dozen signatures on the bookshelf. A scratched-up helmet sat on the corner of his desk, and the entire office was decorated in red and white.

"I graduated class of '78. Go Badgers! I played linebacker all four years. I actually held the school record for tackles my senior year," Lenny said. He toured Scott around his office as he recounted the stories behind each item, and Scott was impressed. He never got into professional football like many of his friends and co-workers did. He was one of those guys who read the sports page just so he at least knew what people were talking about. But he loved college football. Even though he graduated from the University of Central Florida, he was a Florida State University Seminole fan at heart. Every homecoming, he would travel up to Tallahassee and watch the game with his best friend from high school that attended there.

After graduating college at the University of Wisconsin, his uncle got him a job in recycling and scraps metal. By the time he was 30, he had his own scrap metal business that did quite well for him and his family. He married his college sweetheart and had two children: a boy and a girl. After they both graduated high school, and later college, both of them married and had children of their own. That's when Lenny Kawalski decided that he had had enough snow and cold and retired to Florida with his wife. Within six months, he was stir crazy from the boredom and went looking for something part-time to keep him occupied. He talked to fellow Wisconsin alumni in the area and found out about Granted Wishes Village and he applied. Because he believed in the cause so much, he decided to take a full-time position. Within a year, he was promoted to General Manager of the resort.

Lenny sat down in his chair, and Scott followed suit in the chair opposite Lenny's desk.

"So, here are the keys to the place. They open the game room, movie theater, main offices, and the ice cream shop. The restaurant has a different set of keys, and the Administration building is open 24 hours a day, 7 days a week, 365 days a year. Here's your radio and our code book." Lenny Kawalski reached behind him and grabbed a small binder and handed it to Scott. "To make your life here easier, I suggest you look it over. From six am to eight am is check in at the gate. We have lots of volunteers, workers, families, and actors that come on property every day. Make your patrols and otherwise observe and report. It's very quiet out here. The only time things get dicey is when there's a code red. A code red is if there's a situation when a child needs medical attention, someone will call, 'The king is here' on the radio, and there's a protocol to follow. It's in the code book." Lenny pointed at the binder and let the fact set in that sometimes there are emergencies. "Anyways, that doesn't happen that often, thank the Lord above." Even after living in Florida for the last ten years, he didn't lose his Midwest accent at all, and Scott couldn't help but think of the movie *Fargo* as Lenny talked.

"Come on, sport. Let me show you your patrol vehicle," Lenny said. They both got up, and he led Scott out the back of the Administration building to the parking lot. And then Scott saw it. A bright yellow golf cart with a blue plastic Keystone cop hat on the top sat there in front of them. "Officer Friendly" was painted on both sides.

"So, yeah, that there is the 'Officer Friendly' mobile. The board felt that security here shouldn't have a threatening presence, so they came up with this," Lenny said. *The look on the new security guards' faces when they see the patrol cart is always priceless,* Lenny thought, and he chuckled to himself.

"You better hurry up front, sport. It's busy at the gate this time of morning." Scott was going to ask if he could walk to the guard shack, so no one saw him driving around in this ridiculous golf cart, but Lenny turned around and started back to the Administration building.

"Good luck, sport!" Lenny said over his shoulder and left Scott alone with the "Officer Friendly" mobile. *Ok. Let's do this.* Scott Cooper hopped in and pressed the accelerator. The golf cart whined into existence, and he drove to the guard shack.

Every family staying at Granted Wishes Village got a tag to hang from their rearview mirror stating they were guests. The first family pulled up to the guard shack in a rented mini-van, and after five minutes of frantic searching, could not locate the tag. Scott saw a tiny, frail girl in the back seat with an oxygen mask on. She smiled at him and he waved back, and he let the family in. After a while, Scott just started letting everyone in. *Who's going to sneak into this place?* The volunteers started to arrive for work, and Scott flipped the switch and opened the gate. The first group of volunteers was very nice and stopped their cars to say "hello" and introduce themselves. A tan Buick Le Sabre came barreling down the road leading up to Granted Wishes Village. Scott thought for sure the car was going to pass by and continue down Meridian Road but instead she merged right and slowed down to 25 miles an hour. She blew past Scott Cooper and didn't even look at him. He ran out of the guard shack and yelled, "Hey!" but she was already gone.

The next car pulled in and came to a stop. Scott looked at the costume on the seat next to him and said, "You must be the alligator. I'm Scott."

"I, sir, am a crocodile. Look at the head." The man with a bulbous nose and large Adam's apple grabbed the head of the costume for Scott to see. "See the teeth? Alligators only show their top teeth, and this one is exposing the top and the bottom teeth. And look at the snout. See? It's elongated. I always fact check my roles." The man put the crocodile head back on the seat next to him and drove off. Scott briefly dated a theater major in college, so he knew how eccentric they can be. A few more families and volunteers came through when a red 1967 Volkswagen Beetle wheezed to a stop at the guard shack. A man, in his mid-30's like Scott, emerged from the car. He had a full head of black hair combed back and a well-trimmed beard.

"King Leopold at your service," the king said in an exaggerated English accent as he took a bow. Scott smiled because King Leopold was wearing a Police concert t-shirt, cut off blue jeans, and flip flops.

"It comes off across a lot better in costume, I must admit," King Leopold said. Scott introduced himself. The King handed him a card for a free appetizer at Hal Abrams' Dinner Club and Theater, where he performed at night, got the Beetle started on the third try, and drove into

Granted Wishes Village. And then the bear showed up. A beat-up Honda Accord blaring "Natural Mystic" by Bob Marley stopped at the guard shack, and there was a man wearing a bear costume with the head on the seat next to him.

"Hey, I'm the bear, man. Hey…wait…I'm the bear man, man," he laughed. The fact that he smelled like a Brazilian rain forest and Scott couldn't tell if his eyes were open or not lead him to conclude the bear was high as a kite.

"Why are you wearing your costume?" Scott asked.

"I put it on at night and that way I can sleep in an extra 15 minutes," the bear said.

"Why don't you just go to bed 15 minutes earlier?" Scott asked.

"You know, I didn't think about that. You're a pretty smart security dude," the bear replied and drove off. The traffic coming into Granted Wishes Village started to slow to a trickle, so Scott was about to put the gate on automatic and do his patrols when an old, blue Mustang came up to the gate.

"Oh, it's you! Glad to see you're doing better," said the prettiest girl Scott Cooper had ever seen. She had her light brown hair with blond highlights in a bun and wore a tiara. And she looked familiar, but he couldn't place it. She saw the confused look on his face and smiled at him. Then it hit him.

"You're the cocktail waitress from the other night!" Scott blurted out.

"Yep. That's me," she said.

"Were you the one that got me outside?" Scott asked.

"Ding, ding, ding! We have a winner!" she yelled. Scott was getting lost in her green eyes again just like he did a week ago when she was serving him drinks at a strip club called the Pirate's Booty. She pulled out a business card that read, "Princess Tori," Lisicki and handed it to him.

"I also do children's birthday parties," she said and sped off.

✹

Ed Turnbull pulled his brand new red 2001 Ford F-150 King Cab into the parking lot of Gordy's Taco Shop, one of three businesses he owned in the town of Narcoossee, Florida. His associate, Crazy Yaz, stepped out of the cab and went to the back of the pick-up truck. He grabbed a large box out of the back and closed up the tail gate and followed Ed into the restaurant.

"*Bueno Dias*," Ed Turnbull said as he pulled open the doors. Crazy Yaz walked straight back past the counter to the kitchen where Jose Casidilla was chopping vegetables. Gordy's Taco Shop was once a store in a seafood chain called Wuv's that did well during the 70's and 80's but went bankrupt due to over expansion. So, the restaurant sat empty and unused for many years before Ed Turnbull conned the commercial real estate agent into a deal of a lifetime. He replaced the pictures of ships and beaches with paintings of burros and desert landscapes. He took down the anchors and put fake cactus in the corners. Instead of replacing the sign out front, he bought two banners and painted over the "s" in Wuv's, so the sign out front had a banner that read, "You're gonna," and then there was the original Wuv. Then, the banner under it read, "Gordy's Taco Shop." *You're gonna Wuv Gordy's Taco Shop.* Ed thought he was particularly cleaver with the sign, and he saved money. There was only one other restaurant in the area, so Ed Turnbull thought it was a no-brainer. *Besides, who doesn't like tacos?*

"We got another shipment of meat in, Jose. I need you to butcher it up and get it ready for lunch," he said. Jose watched Crazy Yaz pull out a knife from his pocket and open up the box. Inside, on ice, were two dozen headless and tailless rodents known as Nutria. Another name for Nutria is *Louisiana Swamp Grass rat*. Nutria is high in protein and in Louisiana, where everything is eventually thrown into gumbo, it's slowly being served in restaurants. Ed Turnbull heard about it last year at Mardi Gras and was instantly hooked. Not on the taste; he would never eat rat. He was hooked on the price, which was 39 cents a pound.

"It costs me more to ship it than it does for the actual meat," Ed Turnbull joked. Crazy Yaz didn't crack a smile but just stared at the cook. Everything about Crazy Yaz screamed *Russian*. He had jet black hair, gelled back, and he was wearing bright blue running pants, a yellow Gucci t-shirt, and a black leather jacket. And he had a gold chain hanging from his neck. Jose looked with disgust at the box of rats he was expected to pass off as pulled pork. Gordy's famous pulled pork taco combo sold for five dollars, drink not included. But the customer got three tacos, beans, and rice. What was in the tacos was a whole other matter.

"Now, come on, Jose. Don't look like that," Ed Turnbull said. "Do we need to have another conversation about keeping your mouth shut? I'd hate to have to send Yaz here over to your house to hurt you and the misses in front of your children. Then we'll call the authorities and let them know about your family's current legal status in this country. Know what I'm saying, Jose?" Ed Turnbull was about six inches from Jose's face. Crazy Yaz leaned against a cooler and unzipped his jacket to reveal a .38 in the waistband of his running pants. Jose hated the Russian, but he hated Ed Turnbull more. Jose Casidilla was in a precarious situation because he and his family escaped Communist Cuba for Florida. And though Jose loved living in a free country, he still felt "oppressed." There was an understanding between him and Ed Turnbull. Ed didn't require any sort of identification from him to work there. And Ed paid him in cash. Jose then would prep rat before the other employees got to work and keep quiet. And it wasn't like he could call the cops being in the country illegally, so Jose comprised his principles for a better life for his family.

Several years earlier, his brother, a fisherman, agreed to help Jose escape to Florida. He had two inflatable boats built for a backyard pool, not crossing the Straits of Florida, but he was desperate to get his family out. One night, he snuck his family to the docks where his brother kept his fishing boat. His brother took him and his family out as far as he was permitted to go and helped put the two inflatable boats into the water. The water was calm because there wasn't much wind, and the moon was full. His wife and son got into one boat and his daughter and eldest son sat in the other. There wasn't enough room for Jose in either boat without sinking them, so he grabbed each boat by his arms and swam in between them. The water was exceptionally warm as he entered. Jose tried not to think about sharks as he kicked his legs, swimming his family to freedom. Key West is 90 miles due north of Cuba and is actually closer to Cuba than Miami. But the Gulf Stream took Jose and his family north along the coast. After two days in the water, getting stung by jellyfish, and dehydrated, Jose was about to let go of the boats and sink to the bottom out of exhaustion when his daughter cried out. In the distance was Fort Pierce beach. Jose found renewed strength, and his eldest son jumped in the water and together brought the Casidilla family to the United States of America. That's what Jose Casidilla had to endure to get to where he was and now some man was threatening him, like he was back in Cuba. Ed backed away, took a deep breath, and grinned like a used car salesman.

"And we don't want any of those unfortunate events to happen, now do we, Jose?" Jose shook his head. "Good. That's what I thought." Ed Turnbull saw some salsa and grabbed a handful of tortilla chips and dunked them in. When he brought them to his lips, some salsa dripped onto his polo that was struggling to contain the massive beer belly behind it. He carried most of his weight in his midsection and had short legs and a tall torso.

"Now just add some of those Mexican spices to the meat you people use, and no one will ever know." *I'm Cuban, you prick,* Jose thought as Ed Turnbull and Crazy Yaz left Gordy's Taco Shop. Jose Casidilla followed the two men out and watched them drive away. Being Catholic, he knew about God and that judgement would eventually come to wicked men. Until then, he had to accept the fact that every time someone ordered a pulled pork taco combo, he was lying to them. He wasn't poisoning them by any means. And it's probably healthier than the meat served at other fast food places, but still, you're eating rat.

When Dennis Stultzman was a boy, he would come home from school and watch an hour of soap operas with his mother on the couch. It was their ritual. He always liked the characters that were doctors. *They were helping people,* he thought to himself. As he grew up, his ambition to go into medicine became a passion. He graduated valedictorian from Sierra Vista High School in Las Vegas, Nevada. He was quickly accepted at the University of Las Vegas, Nevada where he majored in Biology. He graduated and enrolled in the School of Medicine. After another four years, he graduated and began his residency at Sunrise Children's Hospital. Being a man of routine, he always took his lunch break in the hospital cafeteria at the same time and sat at the same table. He was startled when a voice broke his concentration on the word jumble he was working on.

"Which puzzle are you doing?" the voice said. Dr. Denny Stultzman looked up to see a stunning woman holding her tray of food with a newspaper folded under her arm. Her brunette hair hung to her broad shoulders. She had a very pretty face that didn't need much make up and a cute, marble nose. Dressed in a white, silk blouse, and black skirt, she was one well put together woman.

"Uh…the jumble, I mean, I am working on the word jumble. The paper has them in the classifieds, and I do them every day," said Dr. Stultzman nervously.

"I'll bet you lunch tomorrow I can do it quicker than you can," she said as she sat down opposite him. She took a bite of her sandwich and unfolded her paper to the classifieds. "Go."

Dr. Stultzman was having a hard time with the word jumble today because he was rather smitten with the woman sitting opposite him.

"Done!" she said before Dr. Stultzman had gotten to the fourth jumble.

"Well played. So, if I'm buying you lunch tomorrow, I at least need to know your name," Dr. Stultzman said.

"Lillian," she said and extended her hand as if she was royalty, and without missing a beat, Dr. Stultzman reached out and kissed her on her wrist.

Because Lillian worked in accounting at the hospital, their lunches became a custom. The word jumble always came first and then they would move on to getting to know one another and eat their lunch. After five years, Dr. Stultzman was finishing his residency at Sunrise Children's Hospital. He decided to specialize in child oncology, which wasn't necessarily the top pick of any doctor considering the high mortality rate of your patients, but that's where Dr. Stultzman felt he could do the most good with his talents. He told all of this to Lillian over dinner at their favorite place, *Le Thai*, Freemont Street.

The next day, Dr. Stultzman and Lillian sat down at their usual table in the hospital cafeteria. There was a special word jumble in the paper today that took several weeks for him to set up. As usual, Lillian beat him solving the puzzle and then a confused look washed over her face. The answer to the puzzle was "WILL U MARRY ME?" Right there in the middle of the chaos of doctors and nurses and families with sick loved ones all eating their lunch, Dr. Denny Stultzman bent down on one knee and opened up the box containing a ring that she still wears to this day.

His practice flourished, and on his 50th birthday, he opened The Cancer Institute of Southern Nevada where he was the director and lead physician. Although his career was skyrocketing, there was something missing at home: the pitter patter of little feet. He and Lillian loved each other very much, but after years of trying and all the tests and fertility treatments, they accepted the fact that they couldn't have children. They both rejected the idea of adoption, so they raised black Labradors. For the last 18 years of their marriage, their Christmas photo was always Dr. Stultzman dressed as Santa, Mrs. Stultzman dressed as Mrs. Claus, and the dogs dressed in reindeer costumes.

Vanity plates are very popular in Las Vegas, and to Dr. Denny Stultzman, it was just another word jumble. As they would drive around town on their errands, Dr. Stultzman would frequently yell out, "Lill! I got it! I got! "BNE DR" he's a bone doctor. He's an orthopedist!"

"Yes, dear. Good job," was usually her response, and she would pat him on the leg. One day, they were on the 215, and there was some slight traffic on the southbound. Dr. Stultzman was behind a Ford Expedition that had a license plate "FCSONME," which had him completely stumped. He rolled around a couple of variations in his head, but none seemed right. Then his face brightened, and he turned to his wife of 25 years and said, "Lill! I got it! I got! "FCSONME" is focus on me!"

"Hang on, I'm getting a call from my-" was the last thing Lillian Stultzman said before their BMW plowed at 50 miles an hour into the back of a stopped Expedition. Dr. Denny Stultzman should have been "focusing on me" instead of focusing on telling his wife he had solved another puzzle. He was killed instantly, and Lillian Stultzman spent the next six weeks in the hospital. When she recovered and was released, she held a funeral for her husband and mourned for a month. Then, she woke up one day and took to task settling up her affairs. She sold both houses and the rentals they owned. She received the million-dollar life insurance policy settlement and sold the Cancer Institute of Southern Nevada to the remaining doctors on staff. She took all their remaining assets, which were sizeable on account of her excellent bookkeeping skills and purchased two-hundred acres of land in Central Florida on a lake. She packed up and her and her black lab named "Pepper," moved to a town that took her a week to pronounce correctly.

Within two years of her moving to Narcoossee, Florida, her non-profit organization called Granted Wishes Village was launched. Here, families with handicapped or terminally ill children can come and stay in one of the 150 cottages scattered across the property. There was a full-sized movie theater and a game room with electronic games, as well as skeet ball, air hockey, and pool. There was a restaurant serving breakfast and lunch and a separate ice cream shop. A dock was built out onto East Lake Tohopekaliga that adjoined the property. All free of charge to anyone staying at the resort. Lillian Stultzman supervised the construction, and it was very important to her to have a pool with wheelchair access. And in the middle of the resort was a large carousal, also wheelchair accessible. It was her dream to pick up where her husband had left off, helping children. And because she couldn't heal them, she could at least make their remaining time here pleasant. Her last act before turning Granted Wishes Village over to a Board of Directors was to buy a special bus, so that any family that couldn't afford transportation could travel back and forth to the theme parks in Orlando, 20 miles north.

✳

In 1861, the Civil War began. Florida succeeded from the Union and was a Confederate State. Halfway through the war, the South sent a call for soldiers, and residents of Orlando responded and formed Company A 6TH Florida regiment. The Union attacked, and there was a Confederate victory at the Battle of Narcoossee Mill, where the South fought bravely and won decisively but eventually lost the war.

In 1883, G.B. Smythe was reading the morning paper when an advertisement caught his eye. It detailed the virtues of an area named Narcoossee, which is Creek Indian for "little bear." The ad spoke of acres of farmland, which was perfect for growing citrus. And there was a guarantee that after two years, when the trees matured, $10.000 annually thereafter. So, he packed up his wife and four boys and moved with 200 other English settlers to central Florida.

Narcoossee started as a settlement by a man named C. Nelson Turnbull, Ed Turnbull's great-grandfather. When the settlers arrived, he quickly went out to make sure the town was a success. After much bribery, the St. Cloud and Sugarbelt Railroad was built close to Narcoossee in 1888, which really improved the economy. (Apparently, giving money to elected officials to get what you want has been around for quite some time in the great state of Florida.) Ten years later, the St. Luke Church opened. G.B. Smythe thought, except for all the bugs, he had found paradise for his family. And that's when C. Nelson Turnbull got greedy. There was always shadiness to the man, but the lust for power and more overtook him. In 1910, C. Nelson Turnbull bought 150 square miles in Indian River County for pennies an acre and founded the town of Bullsmere. He uprooted the town and took with him all but a handful of residents of Narcoossee. The church moved, and the community disbanded leaving G.B. Smythe's family and a few others behind. G.B. Smythe never forgave C. Nelson Turnbull for moving the town. And he would pass down the stories of the deception to his son, who would tell it to his son, and so forth.

The centennial celebration of the Civil War was in 1961, and Civil War re-enactments became popular in the eighties. The Battle of Narcoossee Mill became a "four out of five muskets" in the Civil War Re-enactment Newsletter and a "must attend event." The entire town would come out, but no one wanted to be on the Union side. So, they reached out to the Mexican migrant workers who worked the citrus groves to see if they would like to participate, and they agreed. There were occasional incidents of racism in Narcoossee, though never any violence. And it was definitely segregated. The migrants lived to the north in their own little community and kept to themselves while the white population lived to the south. Even though they had to pretend to die, they liked the idea of shooting *Gringos* without getting in trouble. And they didn't have to pay for the dry cleaning of the uniforms.

III

When Ed Turnbull first opened the Pirate's Booty strip club several years ago, he wanted to embrace everything pirate. He had recently stayed at the Treasure Island Casino in Las Vegas and watched the pirate show in front of the casino a dozen times. His original idea was to have the girls dance around a cannon that would fire every hour, but his attorney quickly shot that down after explaining how much insurance an otherwise shady business would have to carry. So, Ed Turnbull turned his attention to creative aspects. The bartenders would dress up in red and blue striped, tight-fitting t-shirts like sailor mates. The cocktail waitresses would wear a white button down shirt, tied in front, a short red skirt, and thigh-high black boots. The uniform also included an eye patch that the girls had to wear. And after the first month, Ed Turnbull saw the cost of broken glassware and split booze and quickly eliminated them. Being in a dark club with flashing lights and only having use of one eye made depth perception an issue.

Scott Cooper walked into the Pirate's Booty, and the smell of sweat and shame hit him at once. He had been to a strip club one other time in his life and that was a buddy's bachelor party. And before he could get his first ever lap dance, the whole group got kicked out and banned for life because the best man bit the nipple of a dancer, and she didn't take to kindly to it. Scott Cooper hoped his second time in a strip club would be better. A couple of mostly naked girls walked by and smiled. However, Scott Cooper wasn't there for a date but to forget about the miserable day he had. He found an empty table and took a seat. A few minutes later, this beautiful woman with light brown hair came up and placed a cocktail napkin down.

"Whatcha drinking, honey?" she asked.

"Maker's on the rocks, double please," Scott replied.

"Stay right here," she said, winked, and walked away. Scott was looking around the room and saw a big guy with blond hair and a smaller Eastern European looking man sitting in the Pirate's Loft, the VIP area. The big guy reminded Scott of the Skipper from *Gilligan's Island* but younger. He had two girls, one on each arm, but the other guy just sat there and looked around, clearly not interested in the women around him. Then Scott noticed a girl dancing on stage. She was probably mid-twenties with bleach blonde hair. She wasn't particularly pretty, but she was topless, so it evened out. Scott looked closer at her thigh. He leaned over to the guy sitting next to him.

"Are those fresh stiches in her leg?" Scott asked.

"Yup. That's my cousin. She fell off her quad runner today. Ain't she a trooper fer goin' to work right after a tragic accident?" the guy sitting next to Scott Cooper said. Scott shook his head up and down and moved to another seat as far away from him as possible.

"There you are. You weren't supposed to move, honey," the cocktail waitress said as she placed his drink down.

"Thanks. What do I owe you?" Scott asked as he reached for his wallet.

"Credit card starts a tab," she replied. "So, I have a theory, do you wanna hear it?

"Ok. Lay it on me."

"Guys fall into two categories. They're either a strip club guy or not. You are not a strip club guy. Am I right?"

"Guilty as charged. What gave me away?" Scott asked.

"Even in the dark, I can tell you're blushing, and you're talking to a woman with clothes on, albeit skanky clothes," she said. He laughed and felt his cheeks go warm. He downed his drink, and the cocktail waitress left to get him another. She came back with a fresh drink, and he downed half of it.

"Slow down there. Your day couldn't have been that bad," she said.

"Wanna bet?" Scott replied. "In the course of 48 hours, I've lost my job, my marriage, my family, and my house."

"I'll get you another drink," she said and walked away. *Are her eyes green? I can't tell, but I'm pretty sure they're green. What pretty eyes.* The bourbon was taking effect.

The cocktail waitress returned with his third double, and he recounted the tale of the last 48 hours. Scott Cooper was a teacher at a program for abused and battered teens, and his day started with two boys getting in an argument about who drank the last of the chocolate milk for breakfast. After that was handled, he received three phone calls in a row from angry parents questioning his teaching methods. He couldn't tell them their kids just don't give a shit, so he tried to turn the conversation towards, "the areas of opportunity your son has are many," and "I try to display positive reinforcement in my classroom." *Good job today, Billy. You didn't punch anyone.* Then there was an email from the Headmaster telling him to remove immediately the three maps of the world he put up and to refer to my employee handbook regarding "displaying my political views in the classroom." *Was it the map of the Middle East?*

At the end of the day, a young college intern, who had been shadowing Scott Cooper all day, saw him slumped in his chair with his head in his hands. His desk was piled with papers to be graded.

"Let's get a drink. Looks like you could use one," the intern said. Scott had hardly noticed her with all the chaos of trying to teach emotionally damaged teenage boys. But she had noticed him.

"Come on. Please? Just one. I promise," the intern pleaded.

An hour later, Scott Cooper sat in the parking of a Friday's and called his wife.

"Hey, babe. Yeah, bad day. Getting a drink with some co-workers," Scott said, feeling a little better about the situation because technically he wasn't lying to her. She was a co-worker. And he wasn't trying to have sex with her. He just wanted someone to talk to that understood the challenges of the job. And he didn't want to go through 21 questions with an over jealous wife to do so. So, he didn't mention that the co-worker was a former University of South Florida varsity basketball cheerleader while working on her Education degree. "Yeah, babe. I promise not to be late. See you soon," Scott said.

The first three bourbons were shop talk, the standard bitching. By bourbon number four, he was recounting tales of his loveless marriage to the intern who was all smiles and smelled like vanilla. By bourbon number six, she was nibbling his ear and running her fingers through his hair. And then things go black for Scott Cooper. He woke up the next morning, naked, lying next to her. *Oh my God! What have I done?* He slipped out of her apartment without waking her, got dressed in the stairwell, and stumbled into the parking lot to look for his car. *Did I drive here? Where the hell am I? Ah, there it is.* Scott started his Cavalier and pulled out onto the street that luckily, he knew. He was 15 minutes away from his house, and he had to shower, change, and make it back to work. And he had to convolute some story as to why he didn't come home last night.

His plan was to rush in and act like, "No big deal," and play it cool. Instead, he saw his wife of 15 years glaring at him from the kitchen table, and he folded like a lawn chair.

"Bad oysters," Scott Cooper mumbled and raced to the bathroom. He took his clothes off and jumped in the shower. *Bad oysters? Ok, Julianna knows that I don't like raw seafood, so maybe I'll tell her that the boys wanted me to try some, and it was a bad batch. I ended up with diarrhea in Kenny's guest bathroom all night long.* He got ready for work and raced downstairs. Julianna was nowhere to be found. That's because while he was in the shower, she went through his clothes and found a receipt from Friday's. Seven Marker's on the rocks, three fuzzy navels. And when she smelled his shirt, it wasn't the usual Old Spice smell but vanilla. The makeup on the collar also did not help Scott Cooper's case. She took both to the lawyer who had been secretly working on divorce papers for her for several months. And now she had the proof she needed.

Scott Cooper got to work 30 minutes late and tried to start his day. Then the intern walked in. Scott felt a weight drop in his stomach. She walked up to him and smiled.

"What, no breakfast?" she said and went to give him a kiss. He stopped her and led her into his office and started the talk he had been working on since he got in the car this morning.

"Look, last night was a huge mistake. And I am so sorry. I should've never gone out for drinks. I had a bad day at work and things at home aren't the best, but I am a married man with a 12-year-old son. And you don't want me, trust me. I'm a boring school teacher trying to turn around lives that don't want to be turned around. I swear to you that I don't remember anything from last night other than having cocktails with you. And if I did anything inappropriate, I am so sorry. Please forgive me," Scott said.

"We made out and got naked, but you passed out immediately, and I was tired, so we went to bed. That's all that happened," she said. "And you snore."

"Thank you for being so understanding," Scott replied, and they hugged.

"But I should warn you, you had me take a picture of your ass, and you texted it to the Headmaster with the caption 'kiss this.'"

Scott Cooper was fired by second period. While he was driving home, the Headmaster called the Cooper residence, got Julianna, and asked her to confirm the address for Scott's final check. By the time he got home, all of his clothes were on the front lawn, and his guitar was on fire in the BBQ grill. He had bought that guitar in high school with plans of forming a band and touring the world. And now it was a smoking pile of burnt wood and copper strings. Julianna even had the locks changed. On the front porch, leaning against the door was a manila envelope that had divorce papers for him to sign within the next 30 days.

"And that's how I ended up here," Scott told the cocktail waitress with the pretty green eyes.

"Wow! That's quite a story," she said. By this time, he was on Maker's number seven, but the cocktail waitress had been watering down his drinks since number four.

"Well, I think you are a good guy that made a bad decision. And hopefully you take responsibility," she said. As Scott Cooper slowly got as drunk as he did the night before, his vision started to go fuzzy. *I must be hallucinating.* A very, very small woman dressed up as a pirate wench walked up to him. She was only three feet tall.

"Hey, baby! How 'bout a lap dance? Half-off?" she asked. And that would be that last thing Scott Cooper would remember about his second strip club experience.

✳

The sun was beginning to shine through the pine trees, and Scott Cooper woke up, hugging the tire of a large truck. He was kneeling against it, and his lap was covered in vomit. His head pounded like a drum line, and his tongue felt like wet carpet. As he slowly made his to his feet, he looked down at the tire he passed out on. *Funny, that rust stain on the hub looks like Texas.* The breeze blew, and Scott got a whiff of raw sewage, which caused him to dry heave. On the side of the septic tank pump truck was painted, *Sanitation King.*

Scott Cooper staggered to his car, got in, and did the emergency check. Wallet. Check. Keys. Check. Phone. Check. He reached into his shirt pocket and found his credit card wrapped in the receipt. *Bless her heart, she only charged me for five drinks and didn't give herself a tip.* The bill was $125.

【 IV 】

Skeet and Tahoe met in jail two years ago and had been partners ever since. Tahoe, Lloyd Bergrasser, got his nickname there because he was built like a Chevy Tahoe. At six feet, two inches tall and 222 pounds of muscle, he lived up to it. He had short hair, a large chin, and he had a perpetual five o'clock shadow. Skeet, on the other hand, was a short, stocky man with sandy blond hair and a mustache that never looked all the way grown in. Even though Skeet dropped out of high school, he was the brains of the operation, and Tahoe was obviously the muscle. Their latest scam involved playing pool, which is why Skeet and Tahoe were in the parking lot of Pocket's Bar and Grill.

"Ok. So, you know what to do, right?" Skeet asked.

"Yup," Tahoe said. He truly was a man of few words.

Tahoe entered first, ordered a beer, and got three dollars' worth of quarters. Skeet came in a short time after and sat at the opposite end of the bar. As they had rehearsed in the hotel room they were living in, Tahoe went up to the pool tables looking for a game. Eventually, someone would let him play, and of course, money would be involved. The plan was Tahoe would blatantly cheat, get caught, and then a fight would ensue. Fights draw crowds, and that's what Skeet was counting on as he went through the unattended purses. Tahoe would take a dive, and when Skeet gave the signal, he would shove the other guy and run out of the bar. It was perfect because people love cheering for the underdog and to see a man as big as Tahoe getting his ass kicked for cheating seemed like some sort of cosmic justice. The scam worked two more times until Tahoe's pride got in the way. Everything was going as planned until Tahoe didn't take a dive but instead beat the hell out of the mark and sent him to the emergency room. A young woman went back to get her phone out of her purse to find Skeet holding it and her wallet. She screamed.

Skeet and Tahoe were arrested, again. This time the crime was conspiracy to commit a robbery and an aggravated assault for Tahoe to boot. They did a year on an 18-month sentence and were released. Instead of hanging around Orlando, Skeet thought a change of scenery might be nice, so he and Tahoe walked three blocks to the bus station.

"Two tickets to anywhere. This is what I got," Skeet said as he handed the cashier all the money he had, which was waded up in balls. Then with his other hand, he dropped several coins on the desk, a couple hitting the floor. The cashier looked at Skeet blankly, sighed, and started to flatten out the bills and count the coins.

"You have 27 dollars and 36 cents," the cashier said dryly. "The two of you can get to St. Cloud."

"We'll take 'em," Skeet said, not knowing where St. Cloud is. They got their tickets and proceeded to bus #2365. After everyone was on board, the bus pulled out of the station and drove for 20 minutes. Skeet was about to fall asleep when the bus slowed down and came to a stop.

"St. Cloud!" the driver said.

"You're shittin' me! This is as far as we got?" said a very annoyed Skeet.

Skeet and Tahoe walked and eventually found a convenience store. Tahoe found a newspaper stand and took a screwdriver he found on the way there out of his pocket. He jimmied the coin slot and out poured the quarters. Skeet took them and went inside where he put five beef jerkies and a moon pie in his pocket and paid for a Big Sip Dr. Pepper. When he came out to share the loot with his partner, he saw a fat, blond man cussing up a storm outside of his Ford F 150 parked in the parking lot. Skeet approached him and took a long slurp out of his soda.

"What's the problem, fella?" Skeet asked.

"I locked my fuckin' keys in the got dang pick up!" he roared. "And I got important business to attend to." That business would be a newly hired stripper waiting for him at his house boat.

"Hang on, fella," Skeet said. He walked over to where Tahoe was and got the screwdriver. He then climbed into the bed of the truck, and with one quick "pop," he had the back window pried open. He shimmied through and opened the driver's door.

"There you go. One opened pickup truck," Skeet said proudly. "And getting that there window fixed is gonna be a lot cheaper than a locksmith, I can tell you that."

"Ed Turnbull's the name," Ed said as he extended his hand.

"Skeet. And that's Tahoe," Skeet said as he shook Ed's hand and nodded to the man leaning against the building, stuffing beef jerky into his mouth.

"You boys got a place to stay? I could use men with your talents, and I know an abandoned fish camp on a lake that would be perfect for you two. And you can help me out with a little business venture. Whaddya say?" Ed Turnbull said, grinning that used car salesman smile of his. He thought about their current living situation and agreed. Skeet and Tahoe got in the truck with Ed Turnbull, and he drove them to the fish camp he talked about.

"It's right next to a resort for retards," Ed Turnbull said as he screeched onto Narcoossee Road.

Scott Cooper settled into a routine during his second week of work. Every morning he was at the gate, checking people in. The crazy old woman always sped past him. The bear was always stoned. And the highlight of his day was always seeing Princess Tori. He savored the couple of minutes each day he saw her. One day, he was out on patrol when he got a call on the radio.

"Officer Friendly, this is Admin, over," Marie, the pleasant-sounding receptionist at the Administration building said.

"This is Scott, go ahead," Scott replied.

"Officer Friendly, there is a L10200 at cottage 49. Go to maintenance and get a plunger, over," the receptionist said.

Scott grabbed his code book and locked up L10200. A L10100 is a "snake and/or other reptile in domicile." The next one down was "clogged toilet." *Great.* Scott drove the Officer Friendly mobile to the back of the property to the maintenance building. It was more like a big garage with lawn mowers and power washers and other equipment needed to take care of a resort. The walls were lined with tools, and in the corner was an older black man with salt and pepper hair.

"Excuse me, I'm Scott Cooper. I was wondering if I could borrow a plunger?" The old man turned around and smiled.

"I've been expecting you," he said. "Mr. Lucas." The two men shook hands, and Mr. Lucas led him back to his corner of the shop. He reminded Scott of his seventh-grade shop teacher, from the glasses all the way to his mustache.

"Ah, here it is," Mr. Lucas said. He turned around and touched Scott on both shoulders with the end of the plunger. "I now dub you Prince of the Potty."

"Gee, thanks. So, isn't this more of a maintenance thing and less a security thing?" Scott asked.

"How long have you been here, son?" Mr. Lucas asked.

"I'm on my second week," Scott replied.

"I've been here a *lot* longer than you have, son. Return the plunger when you're finished," Mr. Lucas said and went back to work repairing a garbage disposal.

Scott Cooper drove to cottage 49 and knocked on the door. A young woman opened the door, smiled, and let Scott in. On the couch was the little girl with the oxygen mask that Scott recognized from his first day. She smiled through the mask and waved. Scott waved back.

"It's the one by the kid's room," the young woman said. Scott went back to the guest bathroom and started plunging the toilet. After two minutes, Scott pulled out a water-logged pink bunny. The older brother, who had been watching Scott, ran into the bedroom and slammed the door.

"I found the problem," Scott said as he returned to the living room, holding the wet bunny by the ears.

"Mr. Bun Bun!" the little girl shouted and then started to cough. Her mom went over to her and started rubbing her back.

"Settle down, Erin. Settle down. We'll give Mr. Bun Bun a bath, and he'll be good as new," her mom said, still rubbing her back. Her mom looked over at the man who just entered the room and gave him a wink. The couple had long since learned to buy multiple Mr. Bun Buns, and they were currently on number four with number five in a suit case. The man went over and gave the young woman some pills.

"We might have to go to the pharmacy because Erin's pain meds are low," the dad said.

"That's funny, we had a full bottle yesterday when we went to the park," the mom said.

"Yeah, I don't know," the dad said. He left and went into the back bedroom and returned with an envelope.

"I guess I'll hit the bank while I'm out, I swore we had more money," the dad said as he counted the bills.

"Are you folks missing some things?" Scott asked.

"No, I'm sure with the hustle and bustle of the theme parks, we just got forgetful. We don't vacation much," the mom said. Just because he was curious, Scott went to the sliding glass door that led out to the backyard and looked at the woods beyond. Scott locked the door and tried to open it and it did.

"Did you folks lock this door when you left this morning?" Scott asked.

"I'm pretty sure we did," the dad said. Scott opened the door and looked at the lock, which appeared to have been pried open from the outside.

"Can you check to see if anything else is missing?" Scott asked. The couple went through the cottage and looked.

"If we did get robbed, these were the dumbest criminals in history," the dad said.

"Why do you say that?" Scott asked.

"Well, why didn't they take all the cash? There were two credit cards in the envelope as well. They overlooked her jewelry, which isn't much, granted. And they left all the cameras. Why break into a house and steal a handful of Xanax and $60? I'm sure it's just us being absent minded tourists," the dad said.

"Ok, if you say so. If anything else comes up missing, please call us," Scott said. Then he went and grabbed a broom from the closet and wedged it in the sliding glass door. The couple thanked him, and Scott made his way back to the maintenance garage, but he drove slower than normal. *Something about that doesn't seem right,* Scott thought.

When Scott returned to the maintenance garage to return the plunger, Mr. Lucas was nowhere to be found. He went over to where Mr. Lucas was working on the garbage disposal and saw a cup of coffee with steam still coming off. Scott put the plunger down, and his radio crackled to life. It made Scott jump.

"The king is here! The king is here! 87! 87!" Marie the receptionist yelled.

Scott ran out and got in the Officer Friendly mobile and raced up to the guard shack. He flipped the switch and opened the gate. Then he drove over to cottage 87 and radioed the receptionist.

"Gate is open, and road is clear. At cottage now, over," Scott said.

"Copy," Marie replied. This was Scott's first code red at Granted Wishes Village, and he didn't like it at all. The door to the cottage was open, but Scott didn't go inside. He instead waited for the ambulance that he could faintly hear off in the distance. The sirens got louder and louder until Scott finally saw the orange and white van with the flashing red lights fly through the gate and take a right onto Granted Wishes Circle. The ambulance screeched to a halt and the E.M.T.'s piled out, arguing with one another.

"I can't believe you cut through that open field!" she yelled at him. She was a plump black woman with her hair in a bun.

"I wasn't gonna slow roll through the intersection, JoJo! I saved us time!" he yelled back. He was also plump but had red hair in a pompadour, freckles, and light skin. JoJo was getting the med bag while Perry, the other E.M.T., got the stretcher out of the back.

"I'm driving back to the hospital," JoJo said as they made their way into the cottage.

"Like hell you are," Perry replied, following behind with the stretcher. JoJo got to work taking her vitals and Perry started an I.V. They loaded her unto the stretcher, strapped her in, and headed to the ambulance.

"I'm driving back," JoJo said again.

"What, you think taking 41 will be quicker than my way?" Perry asked. They were on opposite sides of the stretcher going back and forth as to whose route was faster to the hospital.

"Ah, guys, sick kid here," Scott interjected. They loaded the child into the ambulance, and JoJo got inside with the mother. The father herded the two other young children into the rental and followed them out. Scott felt bad for the little girl and her family and said a little prayer under his breath.

VI

After three weeks of small talk with Princess Tori every morning at the guard gate, Scott Cooper finally got up the nerve to ask her on a date.

"Can I wear my tiara?" Tori asked.

"Sure," Scott said. "Do I have to call you 'your Majesty' all night?"

"Your Highness will do," she said and smiled. They agreed to meet later that night at Granted Wishes Village. Scott had talked with Henry, the night security guard, and the plan was to borrow the keys and the Officer Friendly mobile, and he would give Tori a tour of the place while it was closed. At ten pm, Tori's Mustang roared into the parking lot adjacent to the guard shack, and she got out. She was wearing a peach top, blue jeans, sandals, and her tiara. She looked radiant.

"Nice catch," Henry said as he elbowed Scott in the ribs.

"Hi, boys," Tori said, and they both took a bow.

"Your Majesty," they both said in unison. Scott waved his arm to the yellow golf cart. "Your chariot awaits," he said. They hooked arms and walked to the Officer Friendly mobile. Henry opened the gate, and they drove off to the game room to start their first date. After fumbling with the keys, Scott opened the door, turned on the lights, and they entered.

"Wow!" Tori said. "I've driven by this place a hundred times and never been inside. Is that skeet ball over there?" Tori asked.

"Why, yes, it is. Do you play?" Scott asked. He walked over and flipped a switch that brought the game to life. He pressed the button, and the skeet balls rolled into the bin. Scott picked one up and tossed it to Tori. "Here's the wager, loser has to make the milkshakes later. Deal?"

"Ok. But I must warn you, honey, I grew up in Jersey and spent many summers on the boardwalk," she said and winked at him.

"Bring it," Scott replied. After one game, Scott noticed that Tori could pretty much put the skeet ball where ever she wants to, whereas Scott took the "just roll the ball and hope for the best" approach. That and the fact that every time it was her turn, he stared at her perfect tear drop butt made concentrating on the game hard. She schooled him.

"Best three out of five?" he asked, and Tori giggled. After he got humiliated at skeet ball, they moved over to air hockey where Scott had a little bit better luck. All the games were free, so they moved from one arcade game to the next. Space Invaders, Pac Man, Centipede. When they had finished up, Scott turned off all the games, shut the lights out, and locked up.

"That was fun. Thanks. But there was mention of milkshakes, wasn't there?" she asked. She touched Scott on the arm, and he smiled as he felt his cheeks get warm.

"Absolutely," he replied. They drove to the Ice Cream Shop, which was located close to the Administration building, so Scott decided to go in the back door and kept the lights off. He made their milkshakes in the dark and cleaned up afterwards. He then drove them back to the game room, and they sat on a bench by the pond, under the stars. There was some thunder off in the distance of an approaching storm, and the temperature was a perfect 75 degrees.

"So, you said you grew up in New Jersey?" Scott asked.

"Yeah. My dad was in commercial real estate and did really well. I fell in love with theater in high school and took a couple of classes in community college. I really wanted to get into acting, so I moved to Florida and a relative got me a job here. I only work at the Pirate's Booty just to make ends meet until I get my break," she said as she looked up at the stars. Then she turned to him. "Oh, I've been meaning to tell you, even though I work there, I've never been nude, and I never will. And I won't sleep with that fat hog who owns the place, no matter how much he begs me. I just thought you should know."

"Thank you for that, but it hadn't crossed my mind. I know how small this town is, and there really aren't a whole lot of employment opportunities," Scott said.

"And you are welcome, by the way," Tori replied.

"For getting me outside, yeah, thanks again." Scott said, a little embarrassed.

"No, I saved you from Lil Bit," she said.

"Lil Bit? What's a Lil Bit?" Scott asked.

"She's our small person stripper. And when she gives you a lap dance, she picks your pockets. She got caught one time, and she pulled out a taser and shocked the poor guy. She told everyone it was a seizure, but I saw the electricity," Tori said.

"Ok then…thank you for that, too. So, I wasn't hallucinating?" Scott asked, and Tori giggled. They sipped their milkshakes, and Scott changed the subject away from strip clubs. "On your card, your last name is 'Lisicki?' Was that traumatizing as a child?"

"You have no idea. And I've heard all the variations of it, too. During fifth grade, my dad insisted that I took Muay Thai kickboxing to be able to defend myself. I think I was in seventh grade when I was having a bad day, and some kid that I didn't even know came up to me and said, 'Hey Lisicki, suck my dickie.' Well, I turned around, grabbed him by the arm, and flipped him over my shoulder. He had to go to the hospital because I apparently broke a rib when I kicked him on the ground. Here, wanna see," and before Scott knew it, she had picked him up by the arm off the bench they were sitting on and flipped him over. He was flat on his back, staring up at her beautiful, smiling face, trying to catch his breath. "And I have a can of Mace in my purse," she said as she pulled him up off the ground. "So, no funny business, mister!" she said.

"Duly noted," Scott said as he brushed himself off. After he composed himself, they sat back down on the bench.

"So, how are things, Scott?" Tori asked. "It seems like I've been doing all the talking tonight."

"Better. I found a furnished one-bedroom apartment behind Hubba's Grub and Subs, which is within walking distance. So, I have that going for me," Scott said. Tori giggled again and twirled her light brown hair that had fallen out of the tiara.

"Soon, I'll get Carl on my two days off from here. He has to sleep on the couch, but he'll get used to it. He's a great kid, and I love him to death. Julianna is being typical Julianna and demanding everything I own and then some in the divorce. But I do have a budding career in law enforcement," Scott said. That got them both laughing. A breeze blew over the pond, and Scott saw Tori shiver, so he put his arm around her, and she nestled her head on his shoulder. As her was rubbing her arm, he felt something. A bump, but it wasn't a mole; it was under the skin.

"What's this?" Scott asked.

"Oh, that. It's a BB. When we were younger, my brother and I knew this kid named Tyler that had a bunch of pellet guns. We borrowed some and went out into the woods shooting at stuff. You know, just being stupid kids. My father was firmly against firearms of any kind. I mean, he wouldn't even buy my brother a cowboy gun and holster for a Halloween costume one year. Well, my brother shot at a tree, and the BB ricocheted into my arm. It didn't really hurt, but the shock was intense. We were so scared that our parents would find out about us playing with guns that we threw them away and ran straight home. I put a band aid on it and left it, and its been there ever since. It reminds me of my brother," Tori said.

"Oh, I'm sorry. My condolences," Scott replied, trying not to make an awkward moment more awkward.

"No, stupid," Tori said and laughed. "He's not dead. He's a waiter at Tommy Bahama's in Point Orlando. I see him once a week. So, how's Carl doing?"

"I talk to him when I can on the phone. You know, he's really sharp. We were talking the other day, and he was telling me about how he would like to go back in time and maybe change some things along the way. I pointed that time travel is tricky because of paradoxes. He asked me what a paradox was, and I told him that what if he goes back in time and does something to where his mom and I don't meet and thus, don't have him. How could he exist if he was never born? You know what he said to me, 'I didn't think of that.' Not 'I don't understand' or 'could you explain that?' but 'I didn't think of that.' At 12!" Scott was clearly proud. Tori looked at him and shook her head. "You are such a nerd!" They finished their milk-shakes, and Scott drove them to the next stop on the date.

Another one of Scott Cooper's odd jobs was working at a movie theater his senior year of high school. So, he had no problem threading up *Cinderella* when they got to the theater.

"Wow, former educator, projectionist, and security guard. You are a jack of all trades," Tori pointed out.

"Yes and master of none," he countered. He led her downstairs and went to the auditorium. They settled into their seats as the beginning of the movie started to play. Tori leaned over and kissed him on the cheek.

"Thank you for a wonderful time tonight, my Prince Charming," she said.

"Anything for you, your Majesty," he said and held her hand.

When Scott Cooper was in college, he took a summer off to find a job and build up his savings before fall semester. He knew a guy named Jim from Biology class that did aquatic landscaping. Over beers one Saturday, Jim told Scott all about it.

"So, rich people build their mansions on lakes, you see. And just like they need people to take care of the house and groundskeepers for the yard, they need people to clean their beaches on the lakes. That's where we come in. I have a guy that gets us leads, and we get contracts for 'wetland mitigation,'" Jim explained. By the look of his dark tan and the reverse raccoon eyes from wearing sunglasses, Scott knew Jim spent a considerable amount of time outside.

"So what exactly is 'wetland mitigation?'" Scott asked. "You rake beaches all day?" He sipped his beer and put it down to listen to his friend.

"Well, there's a little more to it than that. We maintain the pickerel and iris beds, move plants around, clear out debris, design features. That sorta thing. But yeah, it's super chill, and you're in the water all day. I could use an extra set of hands for the next two months. What do you think?" Jim asked. Scott had done landscaping before, and there weren't dead people in graves involved so he said, "I'm in," and they chugged their remaining beers.

The next morning, Scott was dreaming of a beach on a lake. Crystal-clear watered lapped at the white sand. The sun was shining brightly, and there were two bikini-clad vixens sunbathing on lounge chairs. And Scott was there, with a rake, grinning from ear-to-ear. The alarm abruptly woke him up from the dream, and he got out of bed and went to the bathroom to brush his teeth. He came out and threw on a t-shirt and a bathing suit. After rummaging through his closet, he found an old pair of running shoes that he could afford to ruin. A horn blared from the parking lot, and Scott Cooper embarked on his first day as an aquatic landscaper. Jim was behind the wheel of a pick-up truck with a trailer, and there was another guy with a mouse-like face in the cab with him. The guy with the mouse-like face opened the door and got out, forcing Scott to ride in the middle.

"He's wearing sneakers, for Pete's sake!" the guy said to Jim. "He won't make it to the end of the day."

"Now give him a chance, Devin. I'm sure Scott here will do just fine," Jim said. They drove west of town to Windermere where the really rich lived. They arrived at the mansion, and Jim drove the truck and trailer down the driveway and around to the back of the house, down towards the lake. And it was nothing like the dream Scott Cooper had earlier. No crystal-clear water. No sandy white beach. No girls in bikinis. Instead, the scene was something out of *Land of the Lost*. The lush St. Augustine grass went right to the water's edge, and the water was the color of tea. There were several beds of iris with their purple and yellow flowers in bloom. 20 yards out the water gave way to tall cypress trees with long grey moss hanging from the branches that blocked the sunlight. Jim and Devin sat down on the grass, took off their flip flops, and lit cigarettes that they held loosely in the corner of their mouths; *the white trash dangle.* Then they put these mesh coverings with a rubber sole over their feet, known as aqua socks, and marched out into the water.

"What are you waiting for, Nube?" Devin barked. "Git out in the water and start pulling weeds!"

"Yeah, Scott. I AM paying you by the hour," Jim replied. Scott stood ankle deep in the warm water and shook out of fear. His palms were sweating, and his stomach turned knots. His heart beat out of his chest. Fear. Pure. Unadulterated fear. He didn't want to look like an idiot in front of his friend and especially that jerk Devin. But this place was a breeding ground for alligators, dangerous snakes, and venomous insects. His two co-workers waded out into the dark water up to their waist.

"Hey, where was that kid eaten by the alligator a couple of weeks ago?" Scott yelled out.

"It was three lakes over that way," Jim said, not looking up but pointing east. "Don't worry, they usually sleep during the day and feed at dusk."

"Shit or get off the pot, Nube!" Devin shouted. Scott took a couple of deep breaths and entered the water. He chose the iris bed closest to the shore. A stick brushed up against his leg under water, and Scott jumped. *Ok, if they can do this, you can do this.* Scott took a couple more deep breaths and put his arm into the bed up to his shoulder and started pulling the dead growth out. And nothing happened. Nothing bit him. Nothing jumped out of the water and pulled him under. The fear was all in his head. Scott laughed to himself as he remembered high school history class with Mr. Beliecki and listening to President John F. Kennedy's Inaugural speech when he quoted, "and we have nothing to fear but fear itself." Within an hour, he was flicking Black Widows off his shoulder as he hauled up dead vegetation to the beach. He finished cleaning out the bed he was on when he noticed that he couldn't move his feet. They were imbedded in the mud. He pulled and pulled, and finally, his feet came free, leaving behind his well-worn Nike's. Scott Cooper spent the rest of the day in his wet, muddy socks, but he survived his first day and first summer as an aquatic landscaper.

Henry, the night security guard, needed a favor and Scott, being the nice guy that he was, obliged. It was their wedding anniversary, and Henry wanted to drive up to Orlando for dinner and a show with his wife, so he and Scott switched shifts. Scott sat in the tiny, four foot by ten foot guard shack and read an entire *Rolling Stone* magazine, solved six games of solitaire on his laptop, and ate his brown bag lunch when he realized what Henry had said about the most boring job on the planet. He pulled out his journal and started to write. He had always wanted to write a book but didn't know what to write about. So, he would scribble thoughts and ideas down thinking one day, he would put them all together and have his first novel. After an hour, he put the journal in his back pack.

There wasn't the same activity at night as there was during the day, obviously. Scott was growing restless, so he set the gate on automatic, hopped in the Officer Friendly mobile, and went out on patrol. He checked all the buildings to make sure they were locked after making a chocolate milkshake and practicing skeet ball. He drove around the complex and came to the pool. There was a family swimming but not making a lot of noise. The mom, dad, and sister swam around a boy in a wheelchair as he splashed water at them. Even though it was dark, Scott could make out a smile on the boy's face, which made Scott smile and think about his own son. There were strict hours of operation for the pool area, but Scott Cooper decided that the fun the family was having overruled the closing time of the pool and drove on. Behind the pool area was a gravel path through a pine tree forest that lead to five mobile homes currently being used as storage. Scott Cooper drove down the path with only the headlights of the golf cart lighting his way. He stopped, swatted a mosquito on his neck, and looked around. The mobile homes were arranged in a circle and everything looked normal except for the last mobile home. The door was wide open. Then Scott felt it again. Fear. The same fear he felt the first day of his aquatic landscaping. His hands shook, his heart raced, and his stomach twisted in knots. All of a sudden, all the noise stopped. No crickets chirping. No frogs croaking. Nothing. Scott Cooper, unlike his first experience with fear, was alone and in the middle of the night. *Holy shit, I need to call someone!* Then Scott realized who that person was. *It's me.* He pulled out his tiny flashlight and slowly made his way to the door. He shined the flashlight in the trailer, and all he saw was mattresses. It was so dark, he could only see where the light of the flashlight shown. He could hear the silence; the low ringing in his ears and dust particles fell from the ceiling. Scott Cooper turned to his right and made his way down the hall, investigating the two rooms and the bathroom before making his way to the master. *Ok. See, there's nothing to be afraid. It's just an empty trailer full of used furniture.* That's when a small possum scurried out from underneath a desk in the corner of the room. Scott screamed and ran down the hall and out of the trailer while the possum darted back and forth, trying not to get stepped on. He made it outside and leaned against the Officer Friendly mobile and frantically gasped for air as his heart raced a mile a minute. After three minutes of hyperventilating, Scott Cooper regained himself, drove back to the guard shack, and decided to forgo documenting the event in the log book. He stayed there all night with the doors locked and all the lights on until the sun rose and his relief came. *Most boring job on the planet, my ass!*

【 VIII 】

The alligator, later named Lucille by the local fishermen, broke free of her egg and started chirping with her 40 other brother and sisters. Her mother dug through the mound she made with mud and vegetation and picked up her babies in her mouth. She took them to the water, opened her jaws, and the baby alligators swam out. Lucille and her group, or pod, stayed close to their mother for five months. They learned how to hunt insects and small frogs. She was one of the lucky 20% that would survive being eaten by otters, turtles, wild cats, or other alligators. Lucille was born in East Lake Tohopekaliga, which covered 20 square miles and was six miles in diameter. Boggy Creek was the primary inflow to the lake, and it was linked to Big Lake Tohopekaliga by canal 31. There was plenty of fish, turtles, and birds to feed on. And the hyacinth, lilies, and grand cypress trees made perfect cover for an alligator. When she matured at ten-years-old, she mated and would stay in East Lake Tohopekaliga the remainder of her life. And she only had three legs.

Buck and Grip sat on a dock at East Toho Marina, drinking warm Budweisers. They were a six pack each into the evening when Buck came up with an idea.

"You know, I saw some roadkill on the way here. I betcha we could tie it to a rope and catch us an alligator. There's good eatin' in the tail," Buck said. He was the heavier of the two and sported a large beard and wore round John Lennon glasses. He wore overalls with no shirt underneath and a ball cap with an *STP* logo on the front.

"I heard that," Grip replied as he pissed into the water.

"I got some rope and wire in the truck. And some flash lights. All we need is a boat," Buck said as he looked around the boat docks. "There's one." Buck stood up and stumbled his way to his truck and left. 15 minutes later, Buck returned with a flattened raccoon and a Louisville Slugger he kept in the gun rack underneath his arm.

"Gimme a hand with this, or you don't get no meat!" Buck yelled to his companion. Grip got up and walked the dock to Buck's truck and grabbed the items in the cab. The boat Buck scouted out earlier was a ten-foot aluminum Jon boat with a small outboard. Not your normal vessel for pouching alligators, but Buck and Grip's options were limited as well as their senses. They loaded the gear in the boat and stepped in. With their combined body mass, they came extremely close to maximum weight capacity. After several pulls on the recoil rope, the small outboard chocked and sputtered, and off went the two drunken rednecks in pursuit of an alligator.

Buck piloted the boat along the south shore of East Lake Tohopekaliga, and after 20 minutes, he killed the engine and let the Jon boat coast.

"Grab your flashlight and shine by them cypress trees," Buck said. They both turned on their flashlights and started searching. And they found what they were looking for: two red, glowing eyes staring at them right above the surface of the water. Alligators, like cats, have a Tapetum lucidum or "biologic reflector system." This improves night vision and the result of shining a light in the eyes is glowing, red eyes, or *eye shine*. Grip, who was sitting in the bow of the boat, started tying the rope around the carcass.

"And make sure to tie off the other end of that rope. We don't want to lose our supper!" Buck barked.

"I heard that," Grip replied. He stood up, braced his legs on the sides of the boat, and heaved the dead raccoon towards the alligator lurking in the darkness. The dead raccoon splashed and sent the alligator into the water below. Buck and Grip sat in silence and waited. A minute went by. Three minutes went by. Buck was about to tell Grip to pull it in when the boat lurched forward, sending Buck and Grip on their backs in the bottom of the boat.

Lucille was eight feet long at this point in her life and weighed 775 pounds. She sensed the boat approaching and the splash of something in the water. She knew it was food, and she had only eaten once that week, so she ducked beneath the surface to investigate. She swam underneath it, opened her large jaws, and bit into the raccoon. She jerked her head back and forth and went to swim away when there was some resistance. The 'thud' of two objects hitting the bottom of a metal boat resonated through the lake. Lucille tried harder to swim away, but something was holding her back.

"Got Dangit!" Buck yelled as he tried to get up from the bottom of the boat. He got his hands on the side of the boat and pulled himself up. Grip was up on his knees, going for the rope he tied off in the bow. "Grab the damn rope, you moron!"

"I heard that," Grip wheezed.

"Well, just don't hear it, do it!" Buck yelled back. Just as Grip got his hands on the rope, it went slack, and the boat eventually coasted to a stop. Then, Lucille did something that neither Buck nor Grip expected; she doubled back and swam as fast as she could back at the Jon boat. She rammed it with her snout with so much force that it sent the rednecks back into the bottom of the boat. Lucille swam underneath the boat and lunged herself up. Buck grabbed the baseball bat with his right hand and started swinging at her head. He landed two blows that stunned her.

"Quick, get that wire around her leg, so she don't go nowhere!" Buck yelled. Grip got the wire noose around her back leg and tied it off on the kleet. Buck swung the bat over his head to give one last blow when Lucille came to life. She thrashed about, and her massive tail sent up waves of water into the already sinking boat. Lucille jerked and jerked against the wire. And the more she did, the more it tightened on her back leg. In a final desperate attempt, she rolled over and over again until the wire sheared her leg off her body. She swam to the bottom in pain.

The Jon boat Buck and Grip had stolen filled up with water and sank within five seconds. Neither Buck nor Grip had followed safe boating techniques and left the two life jackets back on the dock because they took up too much room. As the two drunken rednecks tried to tread water in full clothes and boots, the beer buzz left them and was replaced with terror. Somewhere below them was a pissed off three-legged alligator. They frantically tried to swim to the shore and slowly made progress. Lucille swam up to the surface and followed Grip slowly. She bit down on his legs and dragged him under. He didn't have time to scream out, so Buck had no idea his companion had been taken. He squirmed like much of the large prey she hunted and eventually drowned like they all do. She let him float to the surface, so she could locate the other one. He was swimming with all his might towards a fish camp that had recently closed. He could see the dock. It was only 50 yards away. *I can make it,* he thought. That's when Lucille swam up from underneath him and bit him in half at the waist. The next day, there was a search party sent out on East Lake Tohopekaliga, looking for Patrick Smythe's fishing boat that had been reported missing. After hours of searching, all they found were floating Budweiser cans by the fish camp and a Louisville Slugger bitten in half.

IX

Scott Cooper met Julianna Martinez in college. She had long, dark hair and smooth olive skin; a real island beauty. And she was shapely. They sat next to one another in Old Testament Survey. What started off as a casual smile turned into talking after class and eventually coffee together. He fell in love with the fact that she could speak perfect English, and then without missing a beat, turn around and speak perfect Spanish whenever she got a call from her mom in Puerto Rico. Somehow, she found out his birthday and got him a card that she wrote a poem in. And she signed it, *love, Julianna*. They started dating soon after. Scott liked going to the movies, and Julianna liked to go out to eat, so they would have dinner and movie nights. She would pick the restaurant, and he would pick the movie. If he picked a bad movie, she would punish him the following week with a restaurant he hated, like ones that served nothing but sushi or complete vegan menus. He proposed to her on one of their dates at a restaurant that he liked, fortunately. They married the following fall. Scott Cooper finished his Bachelor's in English and minored in Biblical Studies and went into teaching while Julianna went into Information Technology and got a job at a website company. Like most marriages, the first couple of years were great. They took vacations and had dinner parties with their friends. They both enjoyed jogging, so an early morning five-kilometer run became a routine for them. Julianna moved up fast in her company and was promoted to management. One morning, while Scott Cooper was reading the morning paper, she broke the news to him.

"We're pregnant," Julianna said as she sat in his lap and smiled. She had just gotten out of the shower and was wearing a bath robe. She smelled like jasmine from her body wash, and her black hair was still wet.

"Wait, what? You're pregnant? We're having a baby?" Scott asked. Panic, excitement, and fear washed over him all at once. *Am I ready to be a father?* Scott Cooper drove to three different pharmacies and bought three different brands of pregnancy tests and returned home. And all three said the same thing: You're having a baby! You're having a baby! You're having a baby! The pink little lines don't lie. Scott sat on the couch in shock as a million thoughts raced through his head. Julianna sat next to him and took his hand.

"We'll be ok, baby. Don't worry," she said, trying to be reassuring.

"Of course, we will. I just wasn't expecting it. I mean we've talked about it, but I just kept telling myself that having a baby was a long way's off. And now it's here. Parenthood." Scott leaned over and kissed Julianna on the forehead.

"We can fly my mom in from San Juan to stay with us. To help out, you know. And your folks live like two hours away. We'll be ok. We're not alone," Julianna said.

"I know we're not," Scott replied. The next several months were a flurry of reading baby books, visiting the pediatrician, and buying baby furniture. They found out they were having a boy, which pleased both Scott and Julianna. For Scott, he had an heir to carry on the family name. For Julianna, boys are just easier. They went through Lamaze class, and it wasn't until Scott was in the delivery room that he realized that the breathing exercise is more for the men than the women. He almost fainted when Julianna went into labor and had to be escorted out by the nurses. Carlos Charles Martinez-Cooper was born at 5:02 am on August 26, 1989. And Scott Cooper was in the hallway on his hands and knees, breathing in and out, trying to think of a happy place and not pass out.

Senora Martinez flew in a week later and stayed with Scott and Julianna for three months. Scott had taken two years of Spanish in high school and could get by with Julianna. But when her mother came, they spoke to one another so fast, it sounded like Spanish machine gun fire. Although he could pick up every now and again, *stupido* and *gringo*. Senora Martinez flew back to Puerto Rico, and they settled back into a routine. Scott worked during the day, and Julianna worked nights. They would hand off Carlos, or Carl as Scott preferred to call him, in between. And unfortunately, like most marriages, they started to grow apart. It started slowly. The date nights became fewer and fewer. Julianna hung out with her work friends on her spare time. And the times Scott did go with her and they got a babysitter, they talked about technical stuff all night long that Scott had no idea about. They were becoming less and less a married couple and more and more like roommates that had a child together. Scott started to resent Julianna over time because she made more money than him and controlled all the finances. She would give him a ten dollar a week allowance and all debit card transactions had to be cleared by her. And it infuriated Scott. Even though she managed to pay off his college tuition, his car, and his credit cards, he still held a grudge. A part of it had to do with the fact that she was just plain better at handling money than he was. Julianna, on the other hand, had grown to loathe Scott's little annoying quirks, like the way he scraped his fork on his front teeth when eating or the gulps of air he took when drinking. The chronic snoring was the last straw, and she made him start sleeping in the guest room. The last year of their marriage, Scott and Julianna slept in separate bedrooms. They were staying together for Carl. And it wasn't the typical fighting, yelling, and throwing things at one another. It was just the opposite. Cold silence.

Scott Cooper lay on the couch of his tiny, one-bedroom apartment when he heard the familiar honk of his now ex-wife's Toyota Four Runner. It was precisely ten am and right on time according to the divorce papers. He got up and went outside to get his son for his first weekend visitation since the divorce. Carl was twelve-years-old currently and growing into a man. He had Scott's hazel eyes and Julianna's tan skin. And he was handsome. Fortunately for him, he inherited her good looks and Scott's quirky personality, which made him popular at school. He was getting out of the car when Julianna rolled down her window. She had her hair in a pony-tail and wore big sunglasses, and Scott had to secretly admit that he still found her attractive after everything she took from him. Which wasn't much considering everything was hers. He got the twin bed from the guest room and his clothes. She got his dignity, his soul, and his faith in women.

"Remember, Monday morning at ten. That's what the papers say," Julianna said flatly.

"I know," Scott replied.

"And child support is due on the 30th," she pointed out.

"You make $100,000 a year, plus bonuses and stock options. I make $14 an hour. Why am I-"

"Because you fucked up and screwed some *punta!*" she barked at him.

"I didn't sleep with her!" he shot back. And then he saw Carl come around the back of the Four Runner. "Look, not in front of Carl."

"His name is *Carlos,*" she said. "I'll pick him up. I don't want you to know where we live." She looked at Carlos and blew him a kiss. Then she rolled up her tinted window and sped out of the parking lot.

"We still live in the same place," Carl said, and Scott laughed. He put his arm around his boy's shoulder, and they walked into Scott's apartment.

"You're ok with the couch until I can improve our living situation, right?" Scott asked over his shoulder as he headed to the hall closet to get some blankets and a pillow.

"That's fine, Dad. You do have a bathroom here, right?" Carl asked.

"Yes, smart aleck. It's down the hall across from my bedroom," Scott replied. He came back to the living room and put the blankets on the couch that came with the apartment. He picked up Carl's backpack and noticed that it was open. He glanced inside and immediately dropped back to the floor.

"Carl! You get your butt in here pronto, mister! What the hell is this!" Scott yelled. Carl came out of the bathroom still zipping up his pants.

"What?" Carl asked as he came into the living room.

"What in the name of God's green earth is this?" Scott Cooper reached into his son's backpack and pulled out a handgun that looked and felt like a Berretta.

"Oh, that. That's a Stalker 1918 gun. It only fires blanks. Look, the muzzle is closed up," Carl said rather nonchalantly. He took the gun from his father and showed him the sealed barrel. Then he released the clip and took out the blank cartridges. "And all it does is make a loud bang." Scott Cooper had spent a vast fortune in the Nerf gun phase of his son's life. Which then lead to BB guns and then to the CO_2 guns that recoiled like an actual pistol. Scott had always been leery of the BB guns, but Julianna assured him that all the boys in her country knew how to shoot guns, and her son wasn't going to be the first who didn't. "I was hoping we could go out and shoot it," Carl said.

"Where did you get this?" Scott said, knowing the answer before he asked.

"Mom. She said it was because I'm the 'sweetest boy ever,'" Carl replied using the air quotes.

"Well, I'm not comfortable with a twelve-year-old boy having a realistic looking gun in my house. I'm going to hang onto it until I can talk to your mother about it," Scott said, taking the gun back from his son.

"I'm almost 13," Carl said under his breath. Scott took the weapon into his room and hid it in his closet. Then he dug around some unpacked boxes in the bottom and found a football.

"Come on, Doc. Let's go throw the football," Scott said.

"Why?" Carl asked.

"It's because we need to talk. And this is how men talk. Women talk over coffee, over lunch, over getting their nails done. Men talk to one another by doing something. Like playing golf or going fishing. My dad talked me out of marrying a girl I had no business being with while we changed the oil in my Chevelle. And I need to talk to you," Scott explained. He'd been working on his talk with his son for over a week at work.

"Couldn't we talk like men while we shoot my blank gun?" Carl asked, always playing the lawyer. Scott punched him in the arm, and the two Cooper men walked out behind Scott's apartment complex to a grassy area. Scott tossed the football, and Carl caught it. He threw a perfect spiral back at his father.

"Nice throw, Doc. So, listen, I'm sure your mom has told you a lot about what happened, and I just want you to know my side of things," Scott said and threw the football back to his son.

"Mom said you fucked up and cheated on her," Carl replied.

"Ok. Yes, I did. But I don't like that word, especially coming from you. Alright, how do I put this…" Scott Cooper was looking for the right words to say.

"Look, Dad, I know you and Mom weren't happy together. Geez, give me some credit. I've caught you many times leaving the guest room in the morning. And I know you and Mom love me," Carl said. He threw another perfect spiral, but it went over Scott's head. He retrieved it and threw a long bomb that bounced off of Carl's hands.

"Yes, we do. Both of us. Very much. And your mom and I want to make sure that you know that even though we have our problems, we still want the best for you and will work together to do so," Scott said.

"I know," Carl replied.

"I had a bad day at work and drank too much. I made a bad decision, and I have to take ownership of that. Do you know what the definition of a man is, Doc?" Scott asked.

"It's a guy with guy parts, right?" Carl asked. He threw the ball to his father.

"It's more than that. It's a man who rejects passivity, leads courageously, takes responsibility, and openly accepts the gifts that God has for him. And I need to take responsibility for my actions. That's why all of this is happening. But we'll be ok. I promise. Time has a way of healing things. Your mom is just really mad at me right now, but I know her, and she needs some time to heal. We both do. Do you trust me, Doc?" Scott asked. He hoped his son understood what he was trying to say.

"Yeah, Dad. I do," his son said. "And I'm smarter than you think."

"Oh yeah, how is that?" Scott asked snidely. It's just like his son to find an angle.

"Well, the way I look at it, I get two birthdays, two Christmas', two Easter baskets, two Halloween treats…"

"Whoa, whoa, whoa!" Scott Cooper threw a bullet at his son's chest that he deflected with his hands at the last minute. Carl laughed, picked up the dropped ball, and he ran to his father.

"Can we have burgers and Grammy's potato salad for dinner? Mom has embraced her Puerto Rican roots since you left. If I eat one more plantain, I'm gonna puke!" Carl said. Scott hugged his son and kissed him on the head. When Julianna's mother was there after Carl was born, the house perpetually smelled like fried food. And that's what Carl's hair smelled like.

"You got it, Doc." Scott smiled at his son and felt positive for the first time in months.

X

Scott Cooper had a great weekend with his son. They played board games, watched movies, and ordered pizza. When he was younger, they would spend hours setting up little green plastic army men and having battles. Scott got him hooked on the *Star Wars* trilogy, and of course, had to buy every action figure there was, no matter how insignificant they were in the movie. But he was older now and into video games. Scott found an old Atari game console at a pawn shop and hooked it up to the T.V. Carl complained of the graphics, but Scott reveled in nostalgia. Exactly at ten am, Monday morning, Julianna was there to pick him up. He watched his son walk out to the white Four Runner, and before he got in, he turned and flashed a peace sign with his fingers. Scott flashed a peace sign back and smiled. That had been their thing all through school. Whenever Scott dropped his son off, they would always give each other the peace sign. Scott returned to his apartment and got the blank gun out of the closet. He went out back behind the apartment complex to the grassy area he and Carl were playing catch. He walked to the edge of the woods and pulled the pistol out. He released the safety and shot it three times in a row.

"Holy shit!" Scott yelled. The gun kicked and sounded like a real gun. He quickly put the gun in his pants pocket and covered up the butt of the gun with his t-shirt. He walked briskly back to his apartment with his head down. He put the gun back in the closet and made a mental note to talk to Julianna about this.

Scott saluted to Henry Weisel as he passed through the gate and made his way to the parking lot. Henry and Scott had formed a friendship over the last two months, even though they only saw each other in passing and really only communicated through the log book. Henry agreed to stay late on Monday mornings, so Scott could get Carl to his mom. And in turn, Scott agreed to switch an overnight shift with Henry, so he could have a normal evening with his wife every other week. Scott didn't particularly care for working overnight, but a favor is a favor. Scott parked his rust covered '88 Chevy Cavalier and walked into the Administration Building. He saw Marie, the receptionist with the pleasant voice, behind the desk on the phone. She had a dirty look on her face.

"No, I'm sorry, Ms. Driskoll, we do not offer babysitting services here. Yes, ma'am…yes, ma'am. I'm truly sorry," Marie said and hung up the phone. "What a rude, unhappy woman she is. She wanted to know if we offered babysitting services, so she could enjoy Disney World. She told me her sick son would just slow her down," Marie said as she shook her head. "Unbelievable." Scott agreed, got his radio and keys, and walked out to the back parking lot where the Officer Friendly mobile was charging. *She wanted to go to a theme park without her terminally child. How low can you go?* Scott thought about Carl and thanked God he was healthy.

Scott was doing his patrols around Granted Wishes Village when he saw a boy in a wheelchair on the front porch of cottage 96. Scott Cooper parked the golf cart and walked up the driveway to the porch where the boy was.

"Hi there," Scott said as he waved his hand.

"Hey," the boy in the wheelchair said He was pasty white and had sandy blond hair. Attached to his wheelchair was a pole with an I.V. bag. There was a greenish fluid in it that ran down a tube taped to his right arm.

"My name is Scott Cooper. What's yours?" Scott asked. "Mind if I sit down?" Scott noticed there wasn't a car in the driveway.

"Sure. My name is Toby. Toby Driskoll," the boy said. Scott Cooper gave him a fist bump and sat down in a chair next to him.

"Are your parents inside?" Scott asked.

"Nope. I'm here with my mom, and she left for the store. But she'll be back," Toby replied.

"Mind if I sit here with you until she gets here?" Scott asked. He remembered the last name from the phone call with Marie. She was the Mom that wanted a babysitter service. And this must be the sick boy "that would slow her down."

"Sure. I was just looking at all the green," Toby said as he looked out to the palmetto scrub and pine trees across the street from his cottage.

"Where are you visiting from?"

"I live in Las Vegas with my mom. But my dad lives here in Florida. Stuart. I remember because of the movie *Stuart Little*. Do you know where that is?" Toby asked.

"I do. I was born and raised there," Scott said. It was great to grow up in Stuart. The Inter coastal Waterway that ran from New Jersey all the way to the keys intersected with the St. Lucie River that led to Lake Okeechobee. And there was an inlet to the Atlantic Ocean with West End, Bahamas 90 miles due east. Scott Cooper had a boat by the time he was ten, and he could visit his many friends that lived on the water. He spent his childhood fishing, water skiing, and boating. One summer, Scott Cooper followed behind his father's cabin cruiser in a 13-foot Boston Whaler with a 25 horsepower outboard. They started in Stuart and went south, down the east coast of Florida to the keys. They spent a week lobstering on the many reefs off of Plantation Key. Then they went up the west coast of Florida to Sanibel Island and docked at South Seas Plantation. Before they arrived in Sanibel, his mother had been riding with him, and they decided to explore one of the many coves that dotted the mangrove shore. The cabin cruiser traveled extremely slow, so they took an excursion. They found a cove and slowed down to find two 30-foot cigarette racings boats tied together with men loading something back and forth. Scott was young, but not stupid, so he quickly turned the boat around and followed behind his father's boat. They traveled across the state, over Lake Okeechobee, and followed the Okeechobee Waterway back to Stuart. It was a trip that Scott will remember the rest of his life.

"Last year, I got to spend eight months with my dad in Stuart. It was great. My dad told me that Mom won a vacation with Aunt Forgy to Indian Springs. I've never met Aunt Forgy, but that's what Dad said. And he took me fishing. And we collected shells at the beach. There was a beach he took me to that had big rocks on the shore and a wooden lighthouse," Toby explained. Scott could tell he was excited about spending time with his dad.

"It's called The House of Refuge."

"Right. Anyways, the waves would come in and shoot water into the air through a hole in the rock. It was awesome!" Toby was making gestures with his hands, showing how the water came out of the blow holes.

Gilbert's Bar House of Refuge was built in the early 1900's and it was one of 20 such structures built along the east coast of Florida. The maritime business thrived at that time and because of the violent storms and shallow reefs, many ships wrecked. The surviving sailors would swim to shore and have refuge. Later, a light house would be built to warn captains of the reef offshore. 100-yards out is the wreck of an Italian ship that came too close to shore, and the rocky reef underneath tore the hull to shreds. During World War II, the army would use the lighthouse as a look-out for Germen U-boats. Old timers of Stuart would tell the tale of a Nazi torpedo hitting the beach, exploding, and sending sand spewing a hundred of feet in the air. And it would also serve as a beacon for returning ships buying illegal liquor from a bootlegger named Bill McCoy.

William "Bill" McCoy was born in 1877 in Syracuse, New York. His father was a brick mason who later served in the Union navy at the Confederate blockade. He enrolled in the Pennsylvania Nautical School and learned the ways of the sea aboard the USS *Saratoga* and rose as high as quartermaster. In 1900, the McCoy family moved to Holly Hill, Florida, which is north of Daytona Beach. Him and his brother started a boat building business and earned a reputation as skilled yacht builders after building vessels for the Carnegies and Vanderbilts. They ventured out further and started a freight business that serviced the east coast. Then Prohibition came, and the business started to suffer because the highways being built up and down Florida made it hard to compete. That's when the brothers decided to go into rum running. They sold everything they had and bought a schooner named *Henry L. Marshall*.

What they would do is sail to the Bahamas and purchase as much rum, whiskey, and wine as the ship would hold. Then they would sail back to the east coast and sell it. After several successful trips, he had enough capital to purchase another schooner that he put under English registry to avoid U.S. laws. Bill McCoy would be known as the inventor of the "burlap," which was a bag that held three bottles on the bottom, with two on top of them with one at the very top, all sewed together in a burlap sack. And the liquor he brought back from the Bahamas was the finest to be had. If asked of the quality of the whisky, the response was, "it's the *real McCoy.*" Bill McCoy became a legend in the smuggling circles because he would boast about not paying a single cent to the mob, the police, or anyone in politics for protection. His operation grew to a fleet of six ships, which put him on the radar of the government. So, Bill McCoy changed his strategy and had his ships anchor three miles offshore in international waters and had boats come to him. Finally, the decision was made to bring in William McCoy, regardless of international waters or not. So, the Coast Guard sent a frigate to engage Bill McCoy. When he refused to surrender, the Coast Guard started firing shells at his ship. His crew pleaded with him to give up, which he did, and he was captured. At his trial, he pleaded guilty, and when he was asked about his actions, he replied, "I have no tale of woe to tell you. I was outside the three-mile limit, selling whisky, and good whisky, to anyone and everyone who wanted to buy." After serving nine months in jail, he moved to Stuart, Florida and invested in real estate, especially marinas. One of his many pleasures later in life would be walking the beach from the House of Refuge to the Stuart inlet and back.

Scott Cooper thought about the House of Refuge and his father taking him there to see the blow holes. The big waves came in the winter, and Scott remembered it being cold, especially if you got too close and the water sprayed you.

"I've seen it with my Dad," Scott said.

"And he used to make me pancakes. He tried to make the pancakes look like Mickey Mouse, but the ears were always wrong," Toby said and chuckled.

"Ears on a mouse are hard with pancake batter," Scott replied, speaking from experience.

"I wish I could be with my dad," Toby said rather solemnly. He got a sad look on his face as his head sank into his chest. There was an awkward silence that seemed to last for eternity for Scott.

"Sooo, what's with the green juice here?" Scott asked. He flicked his fingers at the I.V. bag, trying to change the subject.

"Oh, I got lung cancer," Toby replied and coughed a little into his hand. Just then, a black mini-van pulled into the driveway and screeched to a halt. The door opened and out popped a woman in her late twenties with strawberry-blond hair. She had big ears, big boobs, and pouty lips. She was packing a few pounds, but Scott could see that at one point, she had been very attractive. He could see through the plastic bag from 7-11, and it was full of wine coolers and cigarettes and in the pocket of her shirt were several lotto tickets.

"What are you doing here?" she asked rather defiantly.

"Nothing, ma'am. Just watching your unattended child," Scott replied sarcastically. She didn't pick up on the jab.

"Come on, Toby. Let's get you inside," she said to him, not offering to help wheel him in. "It's time for your meds." She looked over at Scott and sighed. "He's got Leukemia." Scott got a confused look on his face as he looked over at Toby. Toby looked down at his feet in the wheel chair stirrups and rolled into the house.

✳

Scott Cooper met Robert Finnell in high school Spanish class. One day, the entire class had to give a five minute speech about themselves, all in Spanish. Scott wrote his speech down on three by five cards and waited to be called. Robert had completely forgotten about the assignment. When it was Scott's turn, he got up and went up to the podium.

"*Hola. Mi nombre es Scott Cooper. Yo vivo en La Florida…,*" Scott said slowly. Five minutes is five hours when one is speaking in a foreign language not fluent in. Scott needed another minute, so he started the speech all over again. The class had no idea because no one was paying attention. Senora Kelly had no idea because she was concentrating on her stop watch. Finally, Scott hit the five-minute mark, and he threw his notecards in the trash and sat down. Robert was up next, and while Senora Kelly was playing with her stop watch, he leaned over and picked up the note cards Scott had just thrown away.

"You may begin, Roberto," Senora Kelly said.

"*Hola. Mi nombre es Scott*, I mean, *Roberto. Yo vivo en La Florida…,*" Robert said as he winked at Scott Cooper. He ended up doing the same thing and repeating the speech over and over again until his five minutes were up. They were friends from that point on. One would think that after listening to the same twelve sentences over and over again for ten minutes straight, someone would've caught on. But no one did, and "Roberto" ended up getting a higher grade for the speech that Scott wrote.

Scott found out that Robert had been playing the drums since he was in the sixth grade, so he went out, bought a guitar, and started taking lessons. He got to the point where he could play several chords in a row and then eventually songs. Being a beginner, he wasn't that good, but it was so much fun to jam music with someone else. He learned some easy Pink Floyd and Tom Petty songs and Don't Quit Your Day Job was formed. They would practice in Robert's garage because it was detached from the house, and his mom was losing her hearing. They spent hours butchering cover songs and enjoyed every minute of it. Scott wrote a couple of originals, but they were always short and the same chord progression. They often talked of bringing in a bass player, but Scott would always refuse at the last minute, stating it would, "ruin the chemistry." One day after band practice, they went outside to open up the garage and get some air. They jumped in the pool to cool off, and Scott looked at Robert.

"You know what I wish? I wish that I'm known for something like writing a song or a book or something. You know, like saving someone from drowning or pulling someone from a burning car. Just something so that before I die, I can tell my kids I did something in life. Do you know what I'm saying?" Scott asked his friend.

"If you're asking me if the song you wrote titled, "Luv Scud" is any good, my answer is no. It sounds too much like the one you wrote called, "Who's Holding Up the Convenience Store," which is a blatant rip off of Bob Dylan," Robert replied. Scott called him "an ass" and splashed water at him. They continued to play music through high school, and after they both left for college, they would still get together and jam, but Robert sold his drum set when he left, so Scott bought some bongos for him to play on when they got together.

Don't Quit Your Day Job had only one paying gig in the bands existence. Scott's mom was in the Stuart Gardening Club and knew a woman that wanted entertainment for her daughter's Bat Mitzvah, so she recommended her son's band. Robert pleaded with Scott to get a bass player, and he finally relented. Robert knew a guy from physics class that played bass in the jazz band. His name was Ted Dillard, and he was good. It only took two practice sessions for him to have the music down. The night of the gig arrived, and they packed their equipment in the Llama van and drove to Sewell's Pointe, where the Copeland's lived. On the way there, they got pulled over for speeding. The police officer looked at all the equipment crammed into every available space. He saw the two boys in the front, the one in the passenger seat with a floor tom in his lap. The officer asked, "Where's the fire, boys?" and Robert replied, without missing a beat, "We gotta get to the gig!" The police officer looked on the dash and saw a collection of cd's ranging from The Police to Led Zepplin. The officer had played drums in a rock band in college, so he let them go with a warning. They arrived and started setting up their equipment that took over an hour. Robert had two five-piece sets that he put together for the "double bass effect." Scott's father had built them an intricate lighting system that had miles of wire and had 16 different colored bulbs. It took three extension cords and five power strips to get everything working. The main control panel was filled with dimmers and switches that someone would just randomly throw to light the lights. Robert got behind his wall of drums and started stretching. His approach to dressing for the event was purely pragmatic; wear the least amount of clothing possible, so it doesn't hinder you from playing. He wore a bathing suit and a Canadian flag as a do-rag. Ted dressed for jazz band in a suit and tie. Scott wore a Black Flag concert t-shirt and ripped blue jeans. They opened with a protest song against Nancy Reagan's anti-drug slogan called "Don't Say No, Say Thank You," which they played perfectly but didn't go over well with the crowd of teenage girls. They only had eight songs in their set list, so they decided to play a couple over again and also added a three-minute drum solo. When the finale came, an original Scott wrote titled "Who Spanked the Altar Boy," Robert had an old cymbal that was bent that he flipped off the stand and hit the ground. He ran from behind his drum set with lighter fluid and matches and lit it on fire. Both Scott and Robert stamped out the flames while Ted continued to play the song. Then Robert ran back behind the drum set and finished the song. The grandmother fainted and girls screamed. They were quickly handed a check for $25 and asked to leave immediately. Mrs. Cooper ended up doing her gardening on her own after that.

The highest point in South Florida is in Stuart, and it's on the St. Lucie River where it turns south towards the Evans McCrary Bridge. There is a hill made of orange sand that is 150 feet above sea level. At the top of the hill are five palm trees that grew in such a way that no matter where the sun was in the sky, there was always shade. Scott named it the five gods. On the right of the sand hill were several cactus plants, and on the left was rusty barbed wire that ran the length of the hill from top to bottom. What kids would do is take their knee boards up to the top and ride the sand all the way down and skip into the water. The Saturday after graduating high school, Scott and Robert took Scott's family boat out to the five gods with a 1.75 liter of Captain Morgan's Spiced Rum. They spent the day riding down the hill and racing up the sand and swimming. And they got piss drunk and ended up passing out under the shade of the palm trees. There was a warm breeze, and it was another perfect day in south Florida, and the two recent graduates didn't have a care in the world. What Scott and Robert should have cared about was there was the full moon the night before. Because of the proximity to the inlet, there is a tidal flux of three to five-feet between high and low tide. A full moon increases that tidal flux another foot and a half. So, when Scott and Robert woke up several hours later, the sun was beginning to set and the 22-foot Grady White with the cutty cabin and 200 horsepower outboard was 100% beached. This was a problem because high tide wasn't for another six hours.

They raced down the hill and started pushing on the 10,000 pound boat…and it didn't move. Panic gripped Scott like a python, and he thought about the prospects of facing his father at some point in his immediate future.

"Quick! Start digging by the bow!" Scott yelled at Robert. They got on their hands and knees and started scooping wet sand with their bare hands. After 20 minutes, they had managed to turn the bow around to face the water, but the heaviest part of the boat, the stern, was still on dry ground. Scott grabbed a rope off the bow and pulled as Robert got behind and pushed. As boats traveled up and down the St. Lucie River, their wake would roll up on the beach of the five gods, and Scott and Robert would slowly inch the boat back into the water. Finally, a large cabin cruiser came by, and the wake was large enough to totally dislodge the hull. They finally got the boat off the beach and into the water. It took them two hours, and during the process, Robert sliced his right foot open on the sharp oyster beds that lived under the water. Scott got him in the boat and tied his shirt over his foot. There was a five-inch slice from the middle of his foot to his heel. Scott then jumped into the water and continued to push the boat out until it was deep enough to lower the outboard. Robert lay in the back of the boat, holding his foot that started to bleed through the shirt. He raced them back to the dock, where his father was waiting for him.

"Do you know what time it is?" Mr. Cooper asked as he tied off the bow of the boat. It was now officially dark.

"Robert's hurt. Can you take a look at his foot?" Scott said, trying to change the subject. Scott's father took Robert by the arm and helped him out of the boat and unto the dock. He put his arm around him, and Robert limped back to the house while Scott hosed off the blood. Scott made it back to the house just in time to hear Robert scream like he had a hot poker put in his eye. While Scott was cleaning the boat, Scott's father took Robert into the bathroom and told him to put his foot in the sink. He removed the bloody t-shirt and took an entire container of rubbing alcohol and poured it on his foot. Robert didn't speak to Scott for two weeks after the incident, and it took third row Rush tickets for him to finally do so.

Robert Finnell got accepted to Florida State University the following fall and majored in criminology. He received his bachelor's four years later and entered the police academy right after graduation. He was later hired by the Kissimmee Police Department where he did his time on patrol and worked his way up the ladder. He was first paired up with a veteran officer and then he was on his own. He became a tact officer, and later, a training officer. After seven years with the force, he joined the Osceola County Sheriff's Department and was quickly promoted to detective. During that time, Robert and Scott remained friends. They still occasionally attended a Seminole football game, and because they lived close, they still got together once a month to BBQ. Robert was the best man in Scott's wedding, and he was Carl's godfather. And it was Robert that talked Scott into being a security officer, and it was him that got Scott the job at Granted Wishes Village. Robert was sitting at his desk when the phone rang.

"Detective Finnell," Robert answered.

"Robert, hey, it's me," Scott said.

"Hey, man! What's up? Did you have another viscous marsupial attack?" Robert asked and laughed.

"I wish I never told you that story," Scott replied. "Listen, I got a favor to ask."

"Shoot."

"Can you look someone up for me on your data base? Her name is Jessica Driskoll, and she lives in Las Vegas." Scott could hear the typing on a keyboard in the background.

"Ok, let's see…wow. She's a real winner. Conspiracy to commit fraud. Credit card fraud. Petty theft. Looks like she did eight months at Indian Springs State Penitentiary for forging checks," Robert reported. *Ah, Aunt Forgy and a vacation to Indian Springs. Toby's father was a genius,* Scott thought to himself.

"Nevada has a 'three strikes and you're out' program, so the next time Ms. Driskoll screws up, she's going away for nickel. What's going on?" Robert asked.

"I think she's pretending her son is sick, so she can take advantage of Granted Wishes Village," Scott said.

"Can you prove it?"

"No. Well, not now."

"I can come by and ask some questions. You know, be a little intrusive."

"No. That's ok. Because if I'm wrong, I would feel terrible hassling a woman about her sick son just because I have a funny feeling."

"Ok. Let me know. Hey, by the way, Rush is playing at the Orlando Arena in two weeks. Are we going?"

"Do you have a nose like Geddy Lee?" Robert laughed and hung up the phone. His French-Canadian nose and pale skin were always an object of ridicule from Scott. Unlike Scott, who was born and raised in Florida, Robert moved to Stuart when he was a sophomore in high school from Connecticut.

XI

"So, what are you trying to say, mother?!" Ed Turnbull asked rather sternly. He had just recently been expelled from the University of Central Florida for poor grades and lack of attendance, and it was the last straw for Martha Turnbull. He took several years after high school to "find himself," and college was his feeble attempt at getting his mother off his back.

"What I'm saying is you're cutoff. I am not going to support you anymore. You can keep the BMW, and the lease on your apartment is paid through December. Here is the information for a bank account that has your part of the inheritance. And you will not get a penny more," Martha Turnbull said. She blew the steam off of her piping hot Earl Grey tea and took a sip.

"What?! That's so unfair! You paid for Jonathon's and Janeen's college!" Ed blurted out.

"They both graduated with honors. You have been on academic probation since the second semester of your freshmen year, which I might add was when you were 25-years-old," Martha replied. Ed's older brother and sister took after their mother and had athletic builds. They also inherited their mother's hard work ethic. Ed, on the other hand, took after his father. Ed was portly in stature, which partly had to do with genetics. A bigger contributing factor was he hated any physical activity that wasn't sex and had a steady diet of fried food and beer.

"Well, what am I supposed to do?" Ed asked. He got up from the couch and started pacing back and forth in the living room. He looked up and saw above the fire place a large painting of his great grandfather, C. Nelson Turnbull, the founder of Narcoossee. And on the mantle was a framed picture of his late father who had passed away of congestive heart failure many years ago.

"I don't know, Edward. That's for you to decide. It's your life, and you have a much better start than most folks," Martha replied to her son. She felt a little at fault because Edward was the youngest, and therefore, spoiled more than his brother and sister. And then Ed's father passed when he was in high school. Martha assumed that his father's death had something to do with his lack luster grades, but then quickly dismissed the idea because Ed had always been lazy. Tough love is always the last resort for any parent, but Edward Nelson Turnbull had forced his mother's hand. Martha hoped that her youngest son would follow suit after his brother and sister, and something would "kick in," but it never did. Jonathon Turnbull was married with two kids and currently the Vice Principal of Lemon Bay High School. Janeen Turnbull Noble married an anesthesiologist and has three children. She was the founder and president of a non-profit organization that helped underprivileged youth. Ed Turnbull, at 27, had never held a job in his life. *Two out of three ain't bad,* Martha Turnbull thought to herself.

Ed Turnbull grabbed the paperwork and the ATM card off the table and marched out the front door, not saying good-bye. He got into his BMW and screeched out of the long driveway and drove straight to the Grand Cypress Hilton. There he purchased a suite and partied like a rock star for the next seven days. A parade of prostitutes came and went, and he had drunk his weight in whisky, twice. After treating his body like an amusement park for a week, Ed woke up, alone, and a big realization started to sink in. *What in the hell am I going to do?*

Ed Turnbull checked out of the suite and drove to his apartment. The following Monday, Ed thought about selling insurance and signed up for a 12-hour class on life, health, and variable annuities and made it through the first two hours of the class. And he left at the break out of sheer boredom. He then enrolled in real estate school and ended up failing the exam two times in a row. When he got the letter telling him he failed a third time, he was exasperated and went to a hole in the wall bar around the corner from his apartment that catered to college students and drank beer. He was sitting at a table alone, on his fourth Corona, when two guys sat down at the table next to him. They drank their Bud Lights and started talking. And they were apparently not college students.

"So, check this out, Billings. I got this cousin that bought a truck with a trailer, and he goes out and picks up people's yard trash and junk and stuff. Then, instead of taking it to the landfill like you're 'posed to do, he just takes it out in the woods and dumps it. All the money he'd hafta pay at the landfill, he just puts in his pockets," Chuck told his friend. Chuck had his back to Ed, but he could hear the conversation because Chuck did all the talking and was loud. Ed leaned in a little closer.

"Ain't he worried about getting caught?" Billings asked.

"Shit (pronounced *she-it*). He ain't dumb. He's got like five places that he goes on rotation. That's all you need. A place to dump," Chuck answered. Ed leaned back to his table and started thinking about what the rednecks behind him were talking about. He went up to get another Corona, but the bartender was on the phone. He gave the international symbol for "one minute" by raising his finger and started talking.

"Hello, yeah, this is The Triangle Lounge on University. We need you to send a septic truck over right away. Shitter's full, again. Ok…thanks," the bartender said and hung up the phone. A light went on inside Ed Turnbull's head, and his used car salesman grin shined on his face. He had an idea. He put the empty Corona bottle on the bar and raced home. He turned on the computer and started looking for used septic tank pumping trucks. After 20 minutes of searching the internet, he found what he was looking for. A 1983 International T300 pump truck with a 1,500-gallon tank, five speed transmission, and airbrakes. It came with a Masport vacuum pump and had 165,000 miles on it. The seller was asking for 30 grand or best offer. After his debauchery at the Grand Cypress Hilton, he was down to $85,000 of his inheritance money. After the truck, paintjob, and business license, that would leave him with 45 grand to invest in the "business" and hopefully never have to come in contact with any crap, literally or figuratively. Ed Turnbull picked up the phone to start the bargaining process when he came up with the perfect name and slogan. *Sanitation King. Your movements make us move!*

In 1995, the city of Orlando, Florida had a population of 175,000 people. Orange County, where Orlando sits directly in the middle of, is home to several theme parks, a major university, and an international airport. The hotel capacity equals that of Las Vegas, its major competitor for the tradeshow business. Ed Turnbull had taken two business classes in his brief collegiate career, and he knew that starting a business in Orange County meant lots of money, lots of red tape, and lots of bureaucracy. Osceola County to the south, on the other hand, had a combined population of 138,000. It's where all the workers for the theme parks, hotels, and other tourist related businesses lived because of a lower cost of living. Ed found a map in his junk drawer and spread it out on his dining room table. Osceola County was mostly lakes, farmland, and citrus groves. He was looking for a place to set up his operations. And there it was. Barely big enough to be considered a town. It was sitting on a big lake with several smaller lakes around the area. And clear on the other side of the county from its only major city, Kissimmee. *Perfect for dumping,* Ed thought to himself. *It's like I'm destined to be there. Thank you, great-grandfather!*

"So, where are you looking to rent, Mr. Turnbull?" the voice of the agent from Sunny Day Real Estate asked.

"Narcoosee, Florida," Ed replied.

XII

Scott Cooper sat in the guard shack of Granted Wishes Village and thought about Tori. They had been on a few more dates and talked regularly. He had written several poems about her but was afraid to give them to her, so he kept them in his journal. Everything was so far, so good. He was planning his next date with her when the radio crackled to life.

"Officer Friendly!" It was Marie.

"Go ahead for Scott," he replied, refusing to answer back as "Officer Friendly."

"There's a code W101 at unit 96. Go to maintenance, and they'll let you know what to do. Over." Scott grabbed the Code Book off the shelf and looked up code W101. Air conditioning or heat related problem. *Why am I handling maintenance issues?* Scott was starting to get annoyed but wasn't in a position to say anything. Plus, he wouldn't say anything anyways because he really needed this job, and he hated rocking the boat. He drove back to the maintenance garage and entered to find Mr. Lucas bent over his desk, working on another garbage disposal.

"Why, hello, son! How are you?" Mr. Lucas said. He put down his tools and turned to Scott.

"I'm fine, thank you. And yourself?"

"I couldn't be better if I tried." Mr. Lucas smiled, and all the anger Scott had worked up on the way there disappeared. "What brings you to my shop, Mr. Cooper?"

"There's a code W101 at unit 96. What do I do?" Scott asked.

"Ah, a code W101. I bet what happened was one of our guests turned the thermostat down too far and froze the condensers. Take this key to open the fuse box. Reset the circuit breaker, wait five minutes, and turn the thermostat up to 68 degrees. That'll be plenty cold for them," Mr. Lucas said. He reached into his pocket and pulled out a key and gave it to Scott. "If I'm not here, just leave the key on my work bench, son."

"So, explain to me again why this is a security issue and not a maintenance issue?" Scott asked. "I mean, what do you do here?"

"Son, I have been here from the beginning, and I have a very important job. One that I'm afraid you wouldn't understand. At least not right now," Mr. Lucas replied.

"That's a cryptic answer for someone who fixes garbage disposals. This is what you're always doing whenever I come here. I'm the one unclogging toilets," Scott said. He wasn't so much angry as he was confused at this point.

"Sometimes the things God has us do isn't pretty or glorious, but trust me, it's worth it in the end," Mr. Lucas responded.

"Yeah, I know. I got that. I do have a minor in Biblical Studies. I just feel like I'm too unimportant to do anything of significance. You know, one time, when I was a teenager, I explained to my best friend how I wanted to do something great and be remembered for it. Not for the fame or glory, just something to mark in history that I, Scott Dow Cooper, had been here.

But that was then and this is now, and currently I am a struggling single parent whose life is in tatters. I'm a nobody."

"Sometimes those are the people whom God choses for His biggest projects. Remember, Peter was only a fisherman."

"Fair enough. I see your point," Scott said, and Mr. Lucas smiled again.

"So, let's change the subject. I've noticed that Lucille hasn't been herself lately, I think-"

"Lucille? The three-legged alligator?" Scott asked. He had seen her numerous times, sunning herself on a fallen log that was across the dock built onto East Lake Tohopekaliga. She was older now and was 13-feet long and weighed 1,100 pounds.

"Yes, the alligator. I think there is something funny going on up at that fish camp," Mr. Lucas said.

"What fish camp?" Scott asked.

"You know the gate at the end of the road leading out of the back that turns onto East Parkway? The dirt road behind the gate goes about 75-yards to a fishing camp that's been abandoned for the last seven years. The cabins are all run down, and the dock is rotted through, but there's a boat ramp. That concerns me," Mr. Lucas said. "I placed a motion camera at the gate about a month ago. Here's the drive with the footage. Let me know what you think." Mr. Lucas reached into his shirt pocket that had his name embroidered on it and pulled out a flash drive.

"Why me?" Scott asked as he took the drive.

"Well, you are security, right? What do *you* do here, son?" Mr. Lucas asked and winked at Scott. "Isn't this a security issue? Oh, by the way. There are some rotten boards on the dock that I need to replace. I've taped it off, so tell the guests to be careful."

Scott left the maintenance garage extremely confused. *Mr. Lucas pulled the key out of his pocket like he was expecting me. And he just happened to have the flash drive with him? Then again, he probably has a radio, but aren't they on a different chan-*

nel? Scott turned left onto Granted Wishes Circle and made his way to unit 96. He parked the Officer Friendly mobile on the street and walked up to the front door and knocked. Jessica Driskoll swung open the door and snarled. "Finally," she said and walked into the kitchen to fix a drink.

"And a pleasant afternoon to you as well," Scott said under his breath. "Air conditioning problems, I hear?" Scott said louder. Scott looked around the living room and saw several shopping bags full of clothes and shoes. He knew that the charity sets up each family with some spending cash, and she apparently was spending it on woman's apparel. Toby wheeled himself out from the back bedroom and waved to Scott.

"How are you feeling? How's the lung cancer?" Scott asked.

"I've got leukemia. Like mom said," Toby said nervously. Scott noticed the I.V. tube was taped to the opposite arm from when he first met him. Jessica Driskoll returned from the kitchen with gin and tonic in her hand. She was wearing exercise shorts too small and a t-shirt without a bra. Scott looked away, and Toby saw her and coughed into hand. "I feel about the same."

"So, are you going to fix my air conditioner? I live in Sin City, so I know hot. And if I'm not paying for it, I want it like a meat locker in here," Jessica said and drained her drink. She left for the kitchen to fix another, and Scott went to work on unlocking the fuse box. *Enjoy the cold now, lady. There'll be plenty of heat where you're ending up.* And Scott Cooper wasn't referring to Las Vegas.

【 X I I I 】

Scott invited Tori over to his apartment for take-out from Hubba's Grub and Subs, the only other restaurant in Narcoossee other than the taco shop. Scott had the famous pulled-pork tacos once, and after spending an evening on the toilet, never went back. He needed her to help him with the flash drive of videos Mr. Lucas had given him. Julianna had been the computer geek in the family, and Scott could barely operate his email. Among her many talents, Tori Lisicki knew her way around a computer. There was a knock at the door, and Scott answered.

"Hey, honey," Tori said and pecked him on the cheek. She was wearing blue jean shorts that rode high, revealing her long, tan legs and green top that laced over her shoulders. "What's for dinner?"

"I got a meatball sub, chicken wings with the hot sauce on the side, like you like it, and loaded potato skins. And I purchased a lovely 2000 Sutter Home chardonnay, which was highly recommended by the sommelier at 7-11," Scott said. Tori giggled and hugged him. Scott loved the way she smelled, and whenever she left, he would always pick up hints of her perfume around the apartment.

"So, you have some sort of mystery video you want to show me, Officer Cooper?" Tori asked. She sat down at his computer and turned it on. Scott came up behind her and handed her the flash drive. He started massaging her shoulders as she downloaded the videos.

"Mr. Lucas told me the video camera was motion activated. So, we should only see something when it passes in front of the camera, right?" Scott asked.

"Right. Ok, let's see what's out there," Tori said. On the computer screen, video appeared of a black and white stray cat walking by the camera. Then it goes blank. A raccoon walks by. Then it came back and stuck his nose in the camera lens and took a sniff. Mr. Lucas had mounted the camera six inches off the ground right outside the gate.

"Ah, that is so adorable," Tori said.

"Raccoons carry rabies," Scott pointed out. She elbowed him in the stomach. Then a video appeared of a possum. Scott jumped back and yelped. Tori turned around and laughed at him.

"Is that the same killer possum from your scary encounter?" she asked. This is the second time in a week he regretted telling someone that story.

"It can't be. The one I saw was the size of a German shepherd with blood dripping from its teeth." He held up his hands like claws and went to bite her throat. She laughed and pushed him back. He was leaning in for a kiss when something on the video caught his eye.

"Hey, roll that back, would you?" Tori went back and pressed play. There was video of two sets of legs, both wearing blue jeans and wearing boots, walking in front of the camera.

"Did you see that?"

"Yeah. So what?"

"Mr. Lucas told me the fish camp was abandoned and has been for some time," Scott said.

"Again, so what? It's probably some guys going out there fishing or something," she replied.

"Maybe it's nothing. Let's keep watching," Scott said. He went and grabbed a chair and sat down beside Tori at his computer desk. The video comes back on, and it's the same two pair of legs walking back to the fish camp. Then the video goes blank. They watched for another half an hour, and various animals walked by the camera. And then there was video of two sets of legs walking back and forth. Scott was about to tell her to turn it off when the video came back on, and it was night. There was a flashlight pointed at the ground with one set of legs walking by. The fence swings open, and the wheels of a large truck drive by the camera. The video goes blank. Then the exact opposite happens in the video. The wheels of a large truck drive by again, the gate swings closed, and one set of legs with a flashlight walk back to the fish camp.

"What just happened?" Scott asked. "Is there any time coding with the videos, so we can see time and dates?" Tori typed and adjusted some settings.

"There... how's that?" She rolled the video back and pressed play, and now the date and time appeared in the lower left of the video.

"You are amazing," Scott said. They went back and filtered out all the critters and started recording the time and dates of the two guys they named thing one and thing two. Scott looked down at the paper with all of the notes and rubbed his eyes. They had been watching videos all night.

"Do you wanna take a break, honey?" Tori asked.

"Let's just go over this one more time, and we'll go to bed," Scott said.

"So, thing one and thing two leave the fish camp and come back several hours later, every couple of days, sometimes at night. Then, at midnight on Wednesday, August 1st, a large truck drives to the fish camp and leaves 40 minutes later. Thing one and thing two come and go. Then, at midnight on Wednesday, August 15th, the truck comes back and does the same thing. Then thing one and thing two come and go again. What do you think is going on?" Tori asked.

"Roll the last video of the truck coming and going but in slow motion." Tori rolled back the video and pressed play. The truck wheels roll by the camera going to the fish camp. The truck wheels roll by the camera leaving the fish camp.

"Stop. Can you play it again but slower?" Scott asked. Tori changed a setting and played it again.

"Pause it!" Tori stopped the video, and Scott got really close to the computer screen. The only light in the video was from thing one's flashlight and the head lights of the truck. But Scott could make something out. There was a rust stain on the hub of the tire. And it looked like Texas.

"I know what they're doing now," Scott said and grinned from ear-to-ear. *Maybe I'm not the world's worst security guard.* "Those assholes are dumping sewage into the lake. I recognize the tire from the truck I passed out on in the Pirate's Booty parking lot. You know, that night you got me outside. It was a septic tank pump truck. And it had a name on the side…sanitation something." Scott was looking at the ceiling trying to remember.

"It says Sanitation King. That's Ed Turnbull's truck," Tori said and got a serious look on her face. "He's not a man to mess with, Scott. Just drop it."

"I can't drop it! He's ruining the environment!" Scott yelled and saw Tori cower a little. "I'm sorry. I didn't mean to yell at you."

"It's ok. I'm just concerned for you. He has people hurt he doesn't like, Scott. So, please promise me you won't do something stupid. Let the police handle it. Don't you have a friend that's a cop or something?" Tori asked.

"I do. I'll call Robert in the morning," Scott said. "What do you know about this Ed Turnbull?"

"I've heard stories from some of the girls at work about him. I guess he moved here about five years ago, in '95, with his septic tank pumping business. He built the Pirate's Booty three years ago from the ground up. Lil Bit told me he had to borrow some money from the Russian mafia in New Jersey. He missed some payments, so that's why Crazy Yaz is with him," Tori explained. "He works for Ed, but he's also here to keep tabs on him."

"Crazy Yaz? Wait, was Ed Turnbull the fat guy with blond hair sitting in the Pirate's loft at the club the night I was there?" Scott asked.

"Ding ding ding! We have a winner!" Tori said. Scott loved it when she said that. It was one of her catch phrases that she used often.

"And the Russian seated with him would be Crazy Yaz?" Scott asked. He had few recollections from the evening, but that, he remembered.

"Yep! He does Ed's dirty work. But lately, there have been two other guys that I've seen with him. A huge guy built like a barn and another smaller guy with a peach fuzz mustache. They showed up about a month and a half ago. Does that mean anything?" Tori asked.

"Do you think they could be thing one and thing two?"

"Now that you mention it, they always smell like campfire smoke," she replied.

"I really wish you would quit that place," Scott said. He knew she didn't dance there or turn tricks but hated the fact the woman he was slowly falling in love with worked at a strip club. Especially now that he knows there is a much bigger picture.

Tori decided to head home instead of staying over, which was fine with Scott. He was still thinking about everything they learned over the night. He packed up some leftovers and walked Tori to her Mustang. They embraced for a full minute, and he kissed her.

"You promise not to do anything stupid?" she asked. She looked at him with her beautiful green eyes.

"Promise," he said. She got in the car, started the 289 with a roar, and rolled down the window. "See you soon?" Scott leaned into the car and kissed her again.

"Yeah, baby. See you soon. What do you think about driving up to Orlando and getting some real food next week? I'm off Wednesday night." She blew him a kiss, and he watched her pull out of the parking lot of his apartment complex and walked inside. He slumped into the couch, rubbed his eyes, and fell asleep.

"Look, it's not like I don't want to help. I do. But did you physically witness these guys dumping sewage into East Lake Tohopekaliga?" Robert asked.

"Well, no. But come on. What else would they be doing out there at midnight?"

"No evidence, no crime. Sorry, but we can't arrest people because we *think* they're breaking the law. We have to know it," Robert explained.

"What if I brought you some water samples? Would that be enough to launch an investigation?" Scott asked. Robert sighed. Real life detective work was nothing like Hollywood makes it out to be.

"Here's what I'll do. I went to F.S.U. with a girl named Anne. She graduated with a degree in environmental law, and I'll call her up and ask her what she thinks. She's the best in the state. But realistically, by the time they send a team down here to look into it, the most they can do is file a cease and desist order. And that will take months," Robert said. "Are you sure you're not doing this to impress Tori?"

"I'm doing this because it's the right thing to do, Robert! You and I both grew up here in Florida. This is our home, and someone is dumping shit in the lake we swim and fish in," Scott said. He was starting to get upset with him but then he tried a different tactic. "What if you caught them in the act?"

"Well, that's a different story. Do you know when and where they're going to do this again?" Robert asked. For some reason, Robert Finnell could tell his friend from high school was grinning on the other end of the phone.

"I'll touch base in two weeks."

[XIV]

Scott Cooper finished the morning check in and put the gate on auto-matic. He wanted to find the car of the crazy old lady that always sped past him. He climbed into the Officer Friendly mobile and turned right onto Granted Wishes Circle and drove to the volunteer parking lot. As he made his way there, he noticed a boy in a wheel chair. It was Toby. Scott slowed the cart down and parked.

"Hey, Toby! Where are you headed?" Scott asked.

"Mom said I needed some air. She has a boyfriend over," Toby replied. "I wanted to go see the alligator. Will you help me? I don't think I can get up the ramp by myself."

"Of course," Scott said. He got behind Toby and pushed him up the ramp and onto the wooden dock that led out onto the lake. The dock went out 50 feet, then turned left another 25 feet. When he reached the turn, he looked over and saw the tape Mr. Lucas had put up across the railings and five or six rotten boards behind it. They were sagging and looked like they would fall apart at the slightest bit of pressure. Scott parked Toby, and they looked for Lucille. They found her lying on her favorite log in the sun. Her eyes were closed, but she still looked menacing…like a dinosaur from another age.

"Wow! How big is she?" Toby asked. His eyes were as big as saucers.

"13 feet. And she weighs more than a grand piano," Scott answered. "When they mate-" Scott cleared his throat and spoke again. "I mean, when a boy alligator likes a girl alligator, he will slap his head against the water, over and over again. Then, the girl alligator will swim underneath him in circles and blow bubbles. That's how they let each other know they like each other. Then they make baby alligators," Scott said. He felt like a teacher again.

"Cool!" Toby said. They sat there in silence and watched Lucille sleep. A snapping turtle splashed into the water, and an egret flew overhead. It was a typical August day in Florida: hot and humid with afternoon thunderstorms. Off in the distance, the clouds were growing dark, and there was lighting. Even though they were in the shade of the cypress trees, and there was a slight breeze off the lake, they started to sweat. After five minutes, Toby confessed to something that Scott Cooper had a hunch on since the first day he met him.

"I'm not sick," he said.

"I know," Scott replied.

"How?!" Toby turned to him and looked genuinely shocked.

"First, you and your mom have different stories. Second, the I.V. tube keeps going back and forth from arm to arm. Let me guess, Gatorade?"

"Mountain Dew. When I get thirsty, I just suck on the tube," he said.

"Third, you said you lived in Las Vegas, right? Dry heat? You're probably not used to sweating like you are now. And your make-up is coming off," Scott pointed out. Toby rubbed his forehead and wiped off white sweat.

"I'm not in trouble, am I?! Please don't tell my mom! Please!" He screamed, and he was on the verge on tears.

"Relax, your secret is safe with me. I won't say a word, I promise," Scott said. He rubbed Toby's head like he would do with his own son.

"What are we going to do?" Toby asked. *What's this "we" stuff?* Scott thought. And then Toby looked at him, and it sent a shudder through Scott Cooper that shook him to the core. He looked exactly like his little brother, Joey, the day he was stuck on the subway in England when the doors shut, and Scott was 11-years-old. Desperation. Fear. *SAVE ME!*

After Scott witnessed the man steal a woman's wallet and did nothing to stop it, the next station was their stop. Nana was breathing heavily, and his mother was looking after her. They made it off the subway car and Scott did, too, but Joey didn't. They were holding hands when the doors opened, and people started pouring out. There was a wave of humanity exiting the subway car, and Scott lost hold of Joey's hand. The doors shut, leaving Joey behind. The look on his face as the subway car departed the station was the same face looking at Scott now at the dock. He remembered he turned to his mother, who was taking Nana to a bench. He ran to her and told her what happened. He had to do something.

"Scotty, I need you to be a man and go get your brother. I have to stay here with Nana. We'll stay right here until you get back," his mother said. So, Scott waited for the next subway car. After a couple of minutes, a subway car screeched its brakes and slowed to a stop. The doors opened again with people spilling out onto the Underground Station. After waiting for the tide of men and women to exit, Scott walked in with 50 other people and turned around and watched the doors shut. The subway car slowly accelerated and made its way down the tunnel to the next stop. When they got there, Scott saw Joey standing by himself by a trash can. Even though he was eight-years-old, he knew to stay right where he was and wait for someone to come get him. The doors opened, and Scott ran to his little brother. They hugged, and Scott asked if he was ok. The farthest underground Scott had ever been was a hole he dug in the back yard, so he was in unfamiliar territory. He figured if they got on a subway car going in the opposite direction, it would take them back where Mom and Nana were. So, they waited, and a subway car approached going back down the tunnel Scott had just traveled. They boarded, and Scott grabbed the pole with one arm and his little brother with the other. He wasn't going to lose him a second time. The subway car left the Underground station and sped to its next destination, which would be three blocks north of the stop that his mother and Nana were at. Scott and Joey exited the subway car and looked around. All the stations looked the same, with only the name of the street painted on the wall to give any distinction. The street name of this particular station was Thompson Avenue, and Scott remembered seeing Blair Street on the wall before he left to get Joey. He didn't want to make the same mistake twice, so Scott made the decision to walk back to the Blair Street station. They walked up the flight of stairs to the street and looked around. They were lost in a major city in another country, albeit a country where they spoke the same language.

Scott Cooper remembered the streets of London being riddled with garbage because the city had removed all of the trash cans. The Irish Republican Army built bombs and deposited them in the trash cans and set them off. It was fortunate for Scott and Joey because there was a police officer on every corner that they asked for directions. Block by block, they made their way back to Blair Street. On their way, they passed a burnt building with "caution" tape wrapped around the entrance. Come to find out, it was the Iranian Embassy that had just recently been raided by the English S.W.A.T. or S.A.S. Some radicals had taken the embassy workers hostage, so the S.A.S. team stormed the building and killed all the radicals. All of the hostages were freed, but the building experienced some damage in the process. Of all the things they would see on their trip to London, the Iranian Embassy would stick out to Scott Cooper the most. After 30 minutes of walking, they found Blair Street Station. They ran down the stairs and found their mother and Nana sitting on the same bench that Scott had left them on.

Now, there was another innocent child that needed his help. Toby Driskoll looked up at Scott Cooper. "What are we going to do?" And just like the situation in the London Underground, Scott felt the need to do something. He didn't want to fail or talk himself out of it like it was someone else's problem. He spent his entire life letting things just pass right by him; not getting involved. He never stood up to his wife their entire marriage. He would cave in on her every whim and demand. He never stood up for anything he believed in. He wouldn't so much as send a meal back at a restaurant if it was wrong. He certainly hadn't "rejected passivity" like he told his son a man should do. He was 35-years-old and a coward. On that dock, Scott made a decision to change into the man he wanted his son to grow up to be. He looked at Toby and thought about what to do. A flash of lightning in the distance caught his eye and then it came to him. *Three strikes, and you're out!* Scott had a plan.

"I've got an idea, but the timing is crucial. Do you trust me?" Scott asked. Without hesitation, Toby answered, "Yes."

"Ok, you saw the alligator today, and we never saw one another. Go home and pretend you and I didn't have this talk. How much longer are you here?" Scott asked.

"We leave in a week," Toby replied.

"Ok. Just keep doing what you're doing, and I'll let you know what to do when the time is right. Cool?"

"Cool." Scott gave Toby a fist bump, and he pushed him down the dock to the ramp. He got him down the ramp when the receptionist called him on the radio.

"Officer Friendly!"

"Go for Scott," he said.

"There's a code 12 at unit 96. Please respond, over."

"Marie, I don't have my code book with me. Just tell me in plain English what's going on, over."

"Domestic disturbance. And she's already called the police." Scott looked over at Toby.

"What unit are you in again?"

"Take a guess," Toby replied.

"Can you get home by yourself?"

"Yeah. Don't worry about me," Toby said. He wheeled himself onto the sidewalk and slowly made his way back to the cottage. Scott raced to unit 96 to see Jessica Driskoll in the front lawn of the cottage next door to hers. There was a man holding a small dog in his arms, and Jessica was screaming at him and waving her fingers in his face. Scott approached the melee and tried to calm everyone down, which caused Jessica's wraith to fall on him. She was wearing a white bath robe with a Howard Johnson's logo on the left breast pocket and one flip flop. And she reeked of gin.

"I don't feel safe staying next to a peeping Tom like that ASSHOLE over there!" Jessica screamed at Scott. "I demand that you move him to another cottage!"

"I was walking my dog, minding my own business. She's on her porch, smoking a cigarette, and she's topless. I saw her, turned around, and walked away. Ginger needs to go potty!" the man yelled at him. This started the argument all over again. That's when the Osceola County Deputy arrived in his green and white cruiser. He was a Hispanic man, a little taller than Scott, and had a black, well-trimmed mustache. Scott looked at his name tag, and it said, "Cruz."

"So, what's going on?" Deputy Cruz asked. Jessica immediately started with her side of the story while the man with the dog just shook his head. Deputy Cruz wrote some notes in his pad and turned to the neighbor.

"And you?"

"I'm walking Ginger because she hasn't made a poopy since we got here. And I see her," he points to Jessica, "topless on her porch. I turned around and walked away. The next thing I know, this witch is banging on my door with her flip flop," the man said.

"Ok. You," He points to Jessica. "You can't be outside your residence naked." Then Deputy Cruz looked at the man. "And you, walk your dog in the front yard from now on." The two neighbors sulked back into their cottages, and Scott looked in amazement at the officer. Deputy Cruz put is notepad into his front pocket and grabbed his radio.

"Dispatch, this is unit 11. Back on duty, over. N.H.I."

"Copy unit 11. N.H.I."

"What's N.H.I. mean?" Scott asked the deputy.

"No Humans Involved," he replied and got into his cruiser and sped off.

After Skeet broke into Ed Turnbull's F-150, Ed called the newly hired stripper and postponed the tryst until later that afternoon. He then drove to the closest Walmart, which was 30 miles away, and spent $200 on camping gear and a cooler. As they drove back to Narcoossee, Ed told Skeet and Tahoe about his many business ventures in the area and his need of help from time to time. He pulled into the 7-11 at the corner of Narcoossee Road and East Parkway and gave Skeet a 50-dollar bill.

"Go get you some beer and food," Ed said. Skeet returned ten minutes later with a case of Miller Lite, a cartoon of the cheapest cigarettes they sold, two plastic bags of subs, chips, and jerky and a bag of ice. Skeet loaded it in the back of the truck and climbed in the cab.

"Tomorrow, I want you boys to meet me here. I got a job for you," Ed said and backed out of the parking spot. He made his way down East Parkway and turned right at the curve. The road ended at a locked gate and to the left was the back entrance to Granted Wishes Village. Ed pulled a key off of his key ring and handed it to Skeet. He got out and opened the gate and got back in the truck. There was a dirt road with pine tree forest on each side. Ed drove 75 yards, and the forest and palmetto scrub slowly gave way to cypress trees, and they arrived at the fish camp. There were four cabins that sat along the lake, all in disrepair. Two had holes in the roof, and all of them were covered in grey moss. The half-submerged dock that once held the many fishing boats in its years of service was crumbling and rotting. And there was a boat ramp that lead to the lake. Clearly, there had not been anyone out there in years.

"Ok, you boys get settled in, and I'll see you at ten in the morning." Ed pulled out of the fish camp and drove out the way he came. Skeet and Tahoe looked at one another and shrugged. They had lived in worse situations, and it wasn't jail. They explored the cabins and found one to be sturdy enough not to collapse on them in the middle of the night. They set up their sleeping bags and made a camp fire outside. And then they drank beer, smoked cigarettes, and watched the sun set over East Lake Tohopekaliga.

The following morning, Skeet and Tahoe started their long trek to the 7-11. It took them an hour to get there, and they were 15 minutes late. Lucky for them, Ed Turnbull was 30 minutes late. They climbed into the cab; Tahoe sat up front because he was bigger, and Skeet sat in the back. Ed took a left on Narcoossee Road and drove for 20 minutes. He turned left at a stop sign and pulled into a new housing development being built.

"Ok, boys, here's my problem. I've got this pain in the ass health inspector that has a hard on for my taco shop. He keeps failing us for whatever reason. Take those pesticide cans in the back and spray his whole front yard. Here's the address," Ed explained as he pulled out a tiny piece of paper. Skeet took it, and they climbed out of the truck. In the back were two three-gallon tanks with an attached hose and nozzle on each.

"I'll be back in half an hour, and I'll meet you right here," Ed said and took off. Skeet and Tahoe started walking up the street. There were several lots marked with surveying tape and a few had concrete slabs. A couple of houses were in the building phase, and Skeet noted workers pounding away a few streets over. Even though it wasn't noon yet, the July heat and humidity lay on them like a warm, wet blanket. And they started to sweat profusely. The street turned right, and there were three completed houses, all next to one another. There weren't any cars in the driveways, so they figured everyone was at work. And to anyone driving by, they looked like landscapers applying weed killer. Skeet wiped his forehead with the back of his hand and fished for the piece of paper with the address on it. The sweat from his hand dripped on the paper, thus bleeding the ink unreadable. Skeet didn't want to disappoint his new employer, so he and Tahoe went about spraying all three yards with gasoline. By the time they finished the third house, the lush, green St. Augustine grass was already turning brown. Skeet chucked the containers behind a hedge, and they briskly walked back to the meeting place, hoping Ed would be on time. And he was. Skeet explained what happened, and Ed laughed so hard, he spit Dr. Pepper all over the dash.

"Well done, boys! Well done!" Ed shouted. "I'm gonna treat you boys right!" Ed Turnbull drove them to the Pirate's Booty and bought them each a lap dance and all the tacos they could eat.

The next job was right up their alley. Ed picked them up again at the 7-11 a couple of days later. Except this time, it was at night. Ed drove them south on Narcoossee Road and took a right at the flashing red light. Narcoossee was so small; it didn't even warrant a real stop light. Ed drove them to the outskirts of St. Cloud and parked outside a business called Chester's Septic Services. Behind a chain linked fence sat a building with three pump trucks parked outside. They were Sanitation King's only competitor in the area.

"Look here, I bought you boys something," Ed said. He pulled out two eight-inch survival knives still in their sheath. Tahoe pulled out the shiny blade and looked at it. "You boys know what to do with them, don't you?" He turned around, and in the dome light, Skeet saw his patented used car salesman smile. Ed brought some bolt cutters, and Tahoe cut a hole in the fence. And there, they slashed every tire on every truck.

The third job they would do for Ed Turnbull left Skeet unsettled the next day. Tahoe, on the other hand, had a certain moral flexibility. Instead of Ed picking them up, it was his assistant, Crazy Yaz. And it was at night again. Skeet and Tahoe walked up to the 7-11 and found a late model Audi idling in the parking lot. The driver's tinted window rolled down, and a man with greased back dark hair and cold, black eyes looked at the two of them.

"Get in," Crazy Yaz said to Skeet and Tahoe. This time, Tahoe sat in the back because even though he outweighed Crazy Yaz by 50 pounds, he was still afraid of the Russian. They drove in silence with the air conditioning blowing cold air full blast. Even though it was the middle of summer in central Florida, Crazy Yaz insisted on wearing a black, leather jacket. As they drove through the night, Tahoe heard a thumping sound coming from the trunk but didn't say anything. Crazy Yaz turned on a dirt road that led to a citrus grove and drove to the middle where there was a clearing. He stopped the car and turned it off but left the headlights on.

"Get out," Crazy Yaz ordered, and all three men exited the car. Crazy Yaz walked around to the back of the Audi and unlocked the trunk. From the light of the trunk door, they could see there was a man inside with his hands duct taped together and a pillow case over his head. Behind him were two shovels and a flash light that Crazy Yaz reached over and grabbed. He turned around and threw the shovels at Skeet and Tahoe and flashed the light at the ground.

"Dig a hole. But not there or there," Crazy Yaz said. He looked confused, like he was trying to remember where he left his car keys. Then he flashed the light to the left of them. "Over here." Skeet and Tahoe started digging, and after 40 minutes, they were waist-deep. Crazy Yaz sat on the bumper and finished the cigarette he was smoking and tossed it aside. He grabbed the man out of the trunk and got him to his feet. He pulled off the pillow case, and Skeet saw he was duct taped around his eyes and mouth. Crazy Yaz ripped off the tape from his mouth, and the guy started blubbering and crying.

"I'm sorry! I'm sorry! I'll pay him! I promise!" the man shouted. "I owe Ed five grand, I've got half! Cash! At my house! Please!"

Crazy Yaz pulled out a .38 revolver from his waist band, held it to the man's temple, and cocked it.

"Tonight, you will give me half the money you owe him," Crazy Yaz said.

"I will! I promise! I'll pay you!" the man said.

"And you will never cross Ed Turnbull again."

"I won't! I promise! Never again!"

"I know you won't," Crazy Yaz said, and he pulled the trigger. The shot rang out in the night, and the man collapsed to the ground. "Bury him." Tahoe dragged the man to the grave and rolled the body in while Skeet just stared at the ground. He thought for sure they dug the hole just to scare the guy, but he was wrong. So, they buried the man who was killed over a $5,000 gambling debt to their new boss. Skeet had broken many laws in his life of crime, and now, for the first time, he was an accessory to murder. What left Skeet unsettled wasn't the act itself, the guy deserved it. But he still felt conflicted. It was the way Crazy Yaz gave the man a shimmer of hope he wouldn't be shot in a citrus grove in the middle of the night.

Crazy Yaz drove them to the house of the man he had recently shot and ordered them to break in and find the 2,500 in cash. They found an unlocked window in the back and climbed into the house and searched it top to bottom. Eventually, they found it underneath his mattress in a manila envelope. They returned 15 minutes later, and Skeet handed over the cash to the Russian. He counted it and pulled two 100-dollar bills and handed them to Skeet. Then Crazy Yaz drove them back to the 7-11 and dropped them off.

"Next Wednesday. Midnight. Ed says to be at the gate, ready."

Life at the fish camp got boring in between Ed Turnbull's odd jobs. One morning, they went exploring and found a trail by the gate that led them to Granted Wishes Village. They walked past the maintenance garage and snuck to the back of a cottage. When they knew it was empty, Tahoe pulled out his screwdriver and jimmied the sliding glass door open.

"Ok, here's the plan. Pills and cash only. And only take a little bit. That way it don't cause no attention." Skeet went to the bathroom and started looking through the medicine cabinet for pain killers. Tahoe searched the rooms and came back with $60. They left the way they came and closed the sliding glass door behind them. They hit three more cottages before they returned to the fish camp and spent the next three days in a hydrocodone haze.

Wednesday night came, and Skeet decided they shouldn't take any pills that day and stuck to cheap beer. At 11:30 pm, Tahoe grabbed a flashlight and walked the dirt road to the gate. He took the key Skeet gave him and unlocked the chain holding the gate closed. When he saw the lights of a truck make the curve, he opened the gate. Crazy Yaz drove the pump truck through the gate and slowed down long enough for Tahoe to jump on the back. *This is the best dumping site we've used yet*, Crazy Yaz thought to himself. When they got to the fish camp, Tahoe jumped off the back and walked to the driver's door.

"Guide me to the boat ramp, and you guys hook up the hose," Crazy Yaz told Tahoe. Skeet held a flashlight, and Tahoe waved Crazy Yaz down the ramp to the water's edge. Skeet unhooked the hose off the side of the truck and attached it to the nozzle on the back of the tank. Skeet opened a valve and watched 1,000 gallons of raw sewage dump into East Lake Tohopekaliga. When the tank was empty, Skeet closed the valve and unhooked the hose and put it back on the side of the truck. Skeet and Tahoe walked up to the driver's door.

"We do this again in two weeks," Crazy Yaz said and drove the pump truck up the boat ramp and back down the dirt road to the gate. Tahoe jumped on the back and came back 25 minutes later. The smell was awful, and they put up with it the first three times. But the fourth time, Skeet had enough and made the decision to check out Granted Wishes Villages. He and Tahoe walked the dirt road to the trail by the gate. When they got to the back gate, they split up.

"All the tourists are home and in bed by now. No sense trying the cottages. You check out them sheds out back, and I'll look around the maintenance garage. Meet back here in an hour," Skeet told his partner.

XVI

Scott Cooper pulled into driveway leading to Granted Wishes Village and stopped at the guard shack. He was here to work for Henry on his overnight shift per their arrangement. Scott had met the part-time guy a couple times in passing. He seemed nice enough but very quiet and to himself.

"Hey, Rich," Scott said.

"Hey, Scott. You're good to go here. I did note in the log book about a family that noticed some cash missing, as well as some pain pills, but the weird part was everything else of value was untouched. I think the tourists got forgetful. Anyways, you have a good shift," Rich said.

"Thanks, Rich. Let me park my car, and I'll be back," Scott said. As he drove to the parking lot, Scott thought, *That sounds like what happened to that family with the flushed bunny.*

Scott pulled out his journal and started writing down all the things that were happening. After an hour, his hand started to hurt, so he pulled out his laptop. Scott had finished his third game of solitaire and was bored. He brought a lunch, but he wasn't hungry, so he went out on patrol to kill some time. It was a lot quieter at night than during the day, and there was almost no traffic coming in or out of Granted Wishes Village. Scott hopped in the Officer Friendly mobile, turned on the lights, and went out to keep the guests safe and secure. He had made three laps around the complex. The first lap was a legitimate patrol. But then he decided to see how fast he could go around the circle. Eight minutes, twenty-two seconds. The third lap was to see if he could beat that time. And he couldn't. He was about to head back when he realized he hadn't checked the sheds. He could very easily note in the log that he had checked the perimeter without ever going past the pool. He thought about it and his decision on the dock and drove onto the gravel path that led to the sheds.

Tahoe ate three hydrocodone that he fished from his pocket as he walked to the trailers out behind the resort. He was hoping to find some cots for him and his partner. The sleeping bags on the wooden floor of the cabin were getting old. He walked the gravel path, and the pills started to take effect. They made him feel warm inside and just all around good. He walked up to the clearing and saw the five trailers parked in a circle. He chose the one closest to him. Tahoe approached the door and pulled out his screw driver. He was about to pry it open when he decided to try the knob. It was unlocked. He put the screwdriver back in his pocket, grabbed his flash light, and started looking around. He was about to enter the back bedroom when he heard something outside.

Scott Cooper drove his yellow golf cart with the blue plastic top hat out to the storage trailers, back behind the property. Just like his first experience out there, it was dreadfully quiet. There was a partial moon that gave a little light through the pine trees. He scanned the trailers from left to right, and everything was fine. Until he got to trailer number five. The same trailer as before had its door swung wide open. *I'd tell Mr. Lucas to fix this, and he'd probably send me back out here with a screwdriver, hammer, and nails!* Scott laughed at himself.

"Ok, mama possum, fool me once, shame on you, fool me twice, shame on me. Ready or not, here I come." Scott pulled his mini flashlight out of his pocket and made his way to the trailer when someone appeared, whose body took up much of the door frame.

Tahoe heard someone talking outside, and paranoia flooded him like a tidal wave. *Is that the cops? Are they here for me? Do they know about the lake dumping thing? If it's just one, I'll shank him and throw his body in the lake. I'll tell Skeet what happened, and he'll help me.* Tahoe looked out the window at a man in uniform. But he wasn't driving a police car but rather some ridiculous golf cart. Tahoe decided to take care of the police man.

"Uh, stop? Who, uh, what-" was all Scott could get out. The man jumped out of the door and started racing towards Scott. Scott in turn took off running in the opposite direction down the dark, gravel path, back to civilization. He lost his radio ten feet into the chase, and he was sprinting for all he was worth. Scott hated running in high school, but once he graduated, he found a passion for getting a few miles a week in. But in this case, he was running in his work shoes on a rocky, uneven surface in the dark. All he heard was his own feet hitting the ground and his heart thumping in his chest. He turned around, half expecting to see the Neanderthal in his dust, to find him hot on his trail, five feet back. That caused the adrenaline to kick in, and Scott ran as fast as he could to the dock.

"You better hope I don't catch you!" Tahoe shouted. *The little man can run, but he'll get tired soon. And once I get my hands on him, it's over.*

Scott was surprised that a man of his size kept pace with him. He saw the lights for the ramp leading up to the dock and raced for it. He started to get winded, and his legs felt like they were on fire, but he kept running. *I hope this works.* Scott ran up the ramp and onto the dock. He could hear the pounding of the footsteps of the man chasing him, but they were further back. The big guy was getting winded also, so Scott slowed down a little. He needed him close but not too close. When Scott came to the turn in the dock, he darted left and ran towards the tape he could barely see in the faint moonlight. The big guy stumbled a little at the turn but grabbed the railing, pulled himself up, and started after his victim.

This guy's an idiot! He's trapped himself. It's either me or the water. Tahoe ran after the slender police officer onto the dock. He saw him dart left down the dock extension and tried to adjust but had too much momentum and hit the side of the dock. He grabbed the railing and started running again.

Scott Cooper ran as fast as he could towards the yellow tape marked "caution." Ten feet. Five feet. Three feet. When he broke through the tape, he planted his right foot and pushed forward and jumped with the remaining strength that he had. He flew over the rotten boards and landed on the other side. He tried to put his arms up, but he still ended up landing on his stomach. When he hit the dock, the wind got knocked out of him, and he lay there like a fish out of water, gasping for air. Pain ran through his chest with every breath in, and he saw stars. He barely had time to push himself up from the dock when he heard the approaching sound of running boots on wood getting louder and louder. The sound of rotten boards breaking under unstainable weight filled the night, followed by a loud splash.

Tahoe saw the police officer leap into the air and land on the dock. *I've got him now!* Tahoe took out the screwdriver when he felt an odd sensation. It's the same sensation one feels when they are walking down a flight of stairs, and they think they are at the bottom, but there is one more stair. Tahoe put his left foot down and encountered no resistance and fell through the rotten boards into the water below. At first, he didn't know what was happening, but as the water filled his mouth and lungs, he realized he fell through the dock and landed in the lake. He started thrashing about and reached for anything he could get his hands on.

Scott Cooper watched the large man disappear before his eyes with a loud crack of wood and a splash of water. He finally got his breathe back and crawled on his hands and knees to the hole in the dock. He saw the large man flailing his arms about. He looked out on the lake, and he saw what looked like a large log floating towards the dock. "Quick, give me your hand!" Scott lay down on his stomach and extended his right arm.

American alligators *(alligator mississippiensis)* have tiny pits in their skin called dermal pressure receptors, and they cover the upper and lower jaw of the alligator. It makes them very sensitive to changes in water pressure and movement. This helps them know the precise location of their prey, even in complete darkness. Lucille, the three-legged alligator, was out hunting when she sensed activity over by her favorite sunning log. She was 30 feet away, but with several waves of her massive tail, she covered the distance quickly. She slowed down and surfaced.

Tahoe was barely treading water when he saw the police man's face. He was shouting something to him, but Tahoe was too busy not drowning to hear him. Tahoe saw him put his hand down. *If I go, I'm taking him with me!* He reached up and grabbed a hand. He was about to pull down with all his force when he looked up and saw nothing but teeth.

Scott grabbed the large man's hand and started to pull up. He was to his knees at this point, and Scott wasn't sure he could handle the weight of the large man onto the dock by himself, but he had to try. He was making progress when he saw a large alligator lunge up and bite the man on the arm Scott was holding onto.

A Florida State University professor did a study on the bite of an alligator. He did the math and concluded this: the bite of an alligator was equal to tying a rope to a bumper of a mid sized pick-up truck. Then take the other end of the rope and tie it to a person and push the truck out of a parking garage. The "jolt" you would feel as the rope went taunt would be the equivalent force of an alligator jaw biting down. So, when Lucille bit down on Tahoe's arm, it was like a hot knife through butter. She severed it just above the elbow, and he fell into the dark water. She grabbed his leg and swam down to drown him. Tahoe was pulled into the darkness, never to be seen again.

Scott fell on his back, still clutching the large man's hand. He screamed like a little girl and threw the arm into the water. He looked down, and his white uniform was covered in dirt and blood. He got to his knees and crawled over to the hole in the dock and looked at the water below. He watched Lucille the alligator slowly surface, grab the partial arm in her jaws, and disappear back into the water. *I can't believe that just fucking happened!* He lay on the dock for a minute to let everything process. He slowly got to his knees and grabbed the rail to get to his feet. His chest hurt, and his head was groggy, but he decided it would be better if he was not there in a blood-covered uniform. He held the rail and inched his way along the remaining boards back to the other side of the sturdy part of the dock. He walked backwards and looked side to side. He turned around and jogged back to the sheds where he parked his cart. He eventually found his radio and the cart and raced to the guard shack where his first priority was to call Tori.

After letting her prey struggle, it finally drowned, and Lucille took her dinner to a sunken Jon boat, that was her favorite hiding spot, and stuffed it underneath for later. She sensed a splash and swam back to investigate. She came to the surface, grabbed the arm, and swam back to the Jon boat. *Hmmm, an appetizer.*

【 X V I I 】

After an hour and a half, Skeet started to get worried about his partner, so he started walking to the sheds. There was enough moonlight that he didn't have to use his flashlight, which made sneaking around in the dark a lot easier. He walked down the gravel path to the sheds and didn't find Tahoe. *I hope that idiot didn't try and break into a cottage at night by himself. Maybe he's checking out the buildings in the middle.* Skeet made his way to the Granted Wishes Circle and followed it around to the cluster of buildings that were the center of the complex. He saw a pond and started towards it when he heard voices. He stopped and crouched down behind a hedge and looked around. He crawled on his hands and knees and made his way to a patio in between the pond and a building he was using as cover. He saw a man taking off his bloody shirt and talking rapidly to a pretty girl holding some clothes.

"And that's when this huge guy ran after me from the storage sheds. I said 'stop,' but he didn't stop. Do they ever stop? Anyways, he chased me to the docks and …" Skeet listened to the whole story while the security guard put on a clean shirt. The pretty girl hugged him, said something Skeet couldn't hear, and walked away and left him alone. The security guard sat in a chair with his head in his hands. *He killed Tahoe,* Skeet thought to himself. They had been partners in crime for the last couple of years, and Tahoe was the closest thing he had to a friend. *He's gonna pay for what he done.* Skeet contemplated what to do next. The security guard wasn't armed, and he could take him by surprise, no problem. Skeet got up and pulled his knife out that he had attached to his belt. He was about to grab him when the pretty girl came back. She was wearing a white shirt tied in the front, a red skirt, and long black boots. Skeet immediately recognized the uniform. He watched them kiss. The security guard held her hand and walked her to her car. *I know where you work, sweetie.* Skeet watched the girl drive away in her old Mustang. *And I know what you drive.*

Tori Lisicki was an hour late for work at the Pirate's Booty because she had to swing by Scott's apartment and grab him a clean shirt. As she drove to work, she thought about the unbelievable story Scott had just told her. When she got there, the night manager chewed her out for five minutes and sent her on the floor. It was a slow night, and Lil Bit wanted to stay, so Tori left after two hours. She changed into shorts, t-shirt, and sandals and walked out to her car. She thought about what time she needed to get up in the morning for her princess gig when she saw someone leaning against her Mustang. It was dark in the parking lot because Ed Turnbull refused to "waste" money on new bulbs for the lights. *I bet Scott got off early, and he's here to surprise me,* she thought.

"Hey, honey! Did you get off early? Wanna come over for a night cap?" Tori asked. Skeet leaned away from the car and emerged from the shadows holding a knife.

"How about my place?" Before she could reach into her purse, Skeet punched her in the face with his free hand and knocked her out. He loaded her into the Mustang and drove off into the night.

✹

Scott Cooper's eventful night was coming to an end. He was still rattled from everything that had happened but talking to Tori helped. He was going to call his friend Robert and tell him all about it once he got home. All he had to do was the morning check-in at the guard shack and the part-time guy, Rich, would relieve him. Just like every morning, there was a steady stream of volunteers and families entering Granted Wishes Village. The crazy old lady sped past again, and Scott was going to write down her license plate number when King Leopold's Volkswagen slowly rolled through. He waved, and Scott waved back. *I'll get you soon enough, Cruella Dev-ille.* The alligator/crocodile and the bear made their way through the gate, and the parade of cars coming through started to slow. Rich pulled up and rolled down his window.

"So, did anything exciting happen last night?" Rich asked.

"Uh, nope. Situation normal. Everything A.O.K.," Scott nervously re-sponded.

"Cool. Let me check in, and I'll be back," Rich said. He pulled away, and Scott gathered his things. He put his journal away and made a mental note to write down what happened at the dock. Then something occurred to him. *I didn't see Tori*, Scott thought to himself. Rich came back, and Scott went to the desk to turn in his radio. Instead of heading to his car, Scott walked over to the movie theater where the characters changed. He entered the lobby and pushed open the swinging doors that lead to the auditorium. He walked down the aisle and proceeded up the stairs to the stage and went left, behind the curtains. There was a room set aside for the characters to change and relax in between performances. Scott looked over at Tori's make-up table, and none of her things were there.

"Any of you guys see Princess Tori?" Scott asked. The alligator sat on the couch with his costume head beside him. He shook his head no. The bear was in full costume, lying on the floor. He shook his head no. King

Leopold shrugged his shoulders. "Well, if she's running late and shows up, please have the office call me, ok?"

"Sure thing," King Leopold replied. Scott drove to the Pirate's Booty on the edge of town. At nine am, the parking lot was empty except for a few cars, and Tori's Mustang wasn't among them. He got out of his car and looked around and noticed Tori's purse on the ground. He picked it up, and everything was still inside. *So, it wasn't a robbery. It has to be the other guy out at the fish camp.* He, once again, felt paralyzing fear that took control and shook him from head to toe as he thought about some low-life doing God knows what to his girlfriend. He took a deep breath and tried to shake off the anxiety that was building inside of him. He grabbed the mace out of her purse and put it in his pocket. Scott threw her purse in the front seat of his car and raced back to his apartment. Once there, he went to his bedroom closet and grabbed his son's blank gun. He pulled out the empty clip and loaded it with the blanks and ran out to his car. There wasn't much traffic on Narcoossee Road except for a white Chevy Trailblazer that drove like they were looking for an address. He passed the SUV, and Scott drove his beat-up Cavalier as fast as he could. He took the left on East Parkway and sped to the curve and slowed. As he rounded the curve, he saw the gate was open. He slowed down more once he got to the dirt road and made his way to the fish camp to rescue Tori.

❰ XVIII ❱

Scott Cooper approached the fish camp in his car slowly. He saw Tori's Mustang parked by a cabin and then saw her and some man sitting by a fire. Tori's hands and feet were bound with duct tape, and she had a strip over her mouth. And he could see blood leaking from under the tape. Scott parked his car, got out, and put his hands in the air. Skeet got up and grabbed Tori by the arm and got her to her feet. He placed a knife at her throat and got behind her.

"You killed Tahoe!" Skeet shouted. "And there will be retribution!" He pulled Tori close to him and tightened his grip.

"Whoa, whoa, whoa! Slow down! I didn't kill anyone. It was an accident. Why was he chasing me in the first place?" Scott asked. Skeet was groggy from staying up all night, and that made thinking hard. That and the fact he had been on a steady diet of oxycodone and beef jerky for a month and a half.

"Shut up! You and your whore are going to get it!" Skeet shouted back.

"Look, this is between you and me. Why don't you let her go and take me instead? She has no part of this," Scott said. He didn't know if reason or logic was going to work with this guy, so he tried a different approach. "Besides, you don't want her as a hostage. Do you know what her father does for a living?" Skeet looked at Tori and then back at Scott. He shook his head. "He is an agent for the Federal Bureau of Investigation. Feel her arm," Scott said as he rubbed his right arm just below the shoulder showing him where. Skeet rubbed her arm and felt the BB. "That is a microchip that every agent and family member receives. If she doesn't check in at a certain time, they send people out to find her. Do you want the F.B.I. here, my friend?"

"Like them chips in dogs?" Skeet asked. He was confused.

"Yeah, like the chips in dogs," Scott replied. He looked up and pointed to the sky. "There are satellites up there right now triangulating her exact location." Scott looked at his watch. "What time to you have to check in? 11 am?" Tori nodded. "She's got 20 minutes before this place is crawling with cops." Scott was hoping he didn't have to pull out his son's gun because he was afraid that the man holding Tori would call his bluff, considering the barrel was sealed. He had the gun in his waistband with his untucked uniform shirt concealing it.

Skeet didn't have much of a plan on how to avenge the death of his friend. After the incident in the citrus groves, he had come to grip with the fact that some people just have it coming to them. But he wasn't going to toy with them like Crazy Yaz did to his victim. Skeet would take care of this guy and dump his body in the lake. He didn't care that the cocktail waitress from the Pirate's Booty saw his face; by the time she got to the cops, he'd be long gone in the security guard's car. But now this guy is talking about federal agents and satellites and microchips, and it was too much for Skeet to process. A small plane flew overhead, and the paranoia took control. Skeet bent down and cut the duct tape around Tori's ankles and pushed her towards Scott. He hugged her, pulled the tape off of her mouth slowly, and kissed her.

"You ok?" Scott asked her. She looked tired and frightened, but she nodded. He then walked over to Skeet with his hands in the air. Skeet grabbed him and turned him around and placed the knife at Scott's throat.

"You, get!" Skeet looked at Tori and nodded towards the road. While Skeet was interacting with Tori, Scott reached into his pocket and grabbed the mace.

"Take that, you asshole!" Scott, in his haste, had the nozzle pointed in the wrong direction. So, when he raised his hand to Skeet's face and pressed the button, the entire contents released into the palm of his hand with a *hiss.*

"You have to be the world's *worst* security guard!" Tori shouted. And she did something that neither Scott nor Skeet expected. She ran as fast as she could and threw herself at them, sending all three of them to the ground, with Skeet on the bottom. Tori got to her knees, and even though she still had her hands bound, she brought them over her head and swung down and hit Skeet square in the nose. He yelped and blood started pouring out of his nose. Scott rolled off of Skeet and writhed in pain. He was still sore from the dock incident, and Tori hitting him in the chest with her shoulder sent a new wave of pain through his core. Tori crawled over Skeet who was holding his bloody nose and rolling on the ground, and she got over Scott.

"Are *you* ok?" she asked. She was looking at him with those beautiful green eyes. Scott took several deep breaths.

"I think so," Scott replied. Reality was starting to come back into focus, and he remembered the dangerous man with a knife lying on the ground next to them. "Let's get out of here!" They started towards his car, but Scott turned around to see Skeet getting to his feet. Instead, Scott grabbed Tori by the arm, and they started running down the dirt road. Tori gnawed on the duct tape, trying to get her hands free as she ran. When they were halfway to the gate, the gun that had been in Scott's waist band came out and landed in the dirt. For a split second, he thought about turning around and getting it, but Skeet was running right behind them, so he hoped that the guy wouldn't see it. When two shots rang out, Scott thought, *he saw it!*

"Make it to the movie theater! We'll lose him there and call the police!" Scott shouted to Tori. They were at the trail, and they ran behind the maintenance garage and down the sidewalk. All the families were on their way to the theme parks, so Granted Wishes Village was deserted. They made it to the movie theater and rushed past the lobby. Scott pushed open the swinging doors, and they were halfway down the aisle when they heard the doors behind them crash open.

XIX

"Stop!" Skeet yelled. He aimed the gun at Scott and Tori who stood there, 15-feet away. *Please God, let that be Carl's gun,* he thought to himself. He put his arm around Tori and whispered in her ear, "I love you." He then grabbed her and turned his back and shielded her as Skeet fired three shots. For a second, Scott thought he felt bullets going into his back, and he winced out of reflex. But instead of collapsing dead to the ground, Scott Cooper just stood there, holding Tori. Skeet looked at the barrel of the gun, and a confused look came over his face. He hit the gun with the palm of his other hand and then banged it on the seat next to him. He aimed again at the security guard and unloaded the clip. He still just stood there with his back to him. No bullet holes. No blood. *What the hell?*

"Shit!" Skeet was livid. He threw the gun at the security guard and hit him in the neck. He pulled out his knife and started his way towards the couple. *I guess I'll have to do this the old-fashioned way.* Skeet was ten feet away when he heard the doors behind him crash open He turned around slowly and saw 235 pounds of Polish muscle and hate barreling at him full speed. When he was hit, everything went black for the criminal known as Skeet.

Lenny Kawalski was at his desk, sifting through paperwork, when he heard the gun shots. He jumped out of his chair and ran out of his office.

"Marie! Call the police!" Lenny Kawalski ran down the hall and pushed open the back door. He ran across the parking lot to the movie theater and pulled open the doors leading to the lobby. He heard more gun shots. He pushed open the swinging doors to the theater and saw a man holding a knife walking towards Scott and Princess Tori. By reflex and muscle memory, Lenny Kawalski got in his three point stance and took off after the man. He lowered his shoulders and threw open his arms. *There's no way this running back is getting passed me!* He tackled Skeet with so much force, it sent the two of them flying, and they landed at Scott's feet. Lenny Kawalski got up and let out a loud "Wooo!" He pounded his chest three times with his right hand and threw both arms in the air; his signature move from college. He then started jogging up and down the aisle yelling, "Go Badgers!" In his head, Lenny Kawalski could hear a stadium of people cheering and yelling his name, "Len-ney! Len-ney! Len-ney!"

King Leopold, the alligator, and the bear rushed onto the stage. King Leopold looked at the commotion going on below and drew his plastic sword from its sheath. "Charge!" he yelled, and the three characters ran down the stairs to the man lying on the ground. Skeet rolled over and was about to get to his feet when King Leopold started beating him in the head with the sword while the alligator and the bear started kicking him in the ribs. Skeet rolled up into a ball and took the onslaught. When they felt he was sufficiently beaten, they backed off to catch their breath but the bear gave one last kick to the head and then pointed out that in every action movie he's ever seen, the bad guy gets away when the good guys aren't looking. So, the decision was made to put the beaten man in the bear costume and tie him to a seat. When the bear unzipped his costume and got out, he was only wearing his underwear and a dirty tie dye.

"Ew," Tori whispered in Scott's ear. They just stood there, holding each other, watching the events unfold around them. They stuffed the beaten man into the bear costume, and with Lenny Kawalski's tie and King Leopold's sash, they tied Skeet to a movie theater seat. Scott heard a siren in the distance slowly getting louder. A minute later, the swinging doors swung open and in the doorway was Deputy Cruz with his gun drawn. He surveyed the situation and holstered his gun. He looked at the menagerie of people in front of him on settled on Scott.

"Ok, what'd the bear do?" Deputy Cruz asked.

X X

Two days had passed since the incident at the movie theater, and things were starting to get back to normal. Scott remembered that Toby's visit was coming to an end, and his window was closing. There hadn't been any issues since she called the police on the neighbor walking his dog. He drove the Officer Friendly mobile over to unit 96, and once again, found the driveway empty. He got out and was headed for the front door when he heard crying in the back yard. He ran to the back and found Toby, lying on the ground underneath a banyan tree, holding his arm. Scott knelt by Toby and did a quick look over.

"You ok, bud? What happened?" Scott asked. "Where's your mom?" Toby looked up at Scott with big tears streaming down his face.

"Mom is at Disney selling our tickets in the parking lot!" he proclaimed. In between sobs, he continued his story. "I just wanted to do something before I left here. I've been in the house watching T.V. the whole time, and I do that at home!" Scott looked up at the thick branches of the 30-foot tall tree overhead.

"How far did you get?" Scott asked. He grew up climbing trees and knew the experience well. He also knew about falling out of trees. When he was in the third grade, he climbed a eucalyptus tree by the side of the house and fell. He hit his head on the corner of the air conditioner. It didn't hurt, so Scott got up and headed for the front door. On his way, he stopped to tie his shoe and blood gushed out of his head. He freaked out and ran inside. His mom was making stuffed bell peppers in the kitchen when Scott came in. There was a hole in his forehead, right at the hair line. She used her hands to pull the hair back and looked at his wound. They ended up going to the hospital, and Scott received six stitches. The doctor performing the procedure wanted to call Child Protective Services because during her inspection of her son's wound, some rice ended up in his hair from the stuffed peppers, and the doctor thought it was fly larvae and the wound had existed for some time. After she and her husband explained the situation, the doctor reluctantly let Scott go home.

"Third branch from the top," Toby replied. *Impressive*, Scott thought. Scott concluded that Toby fell and landed on his arm on the enormous roots of the huge tree. And it was probably broken. He couldn't take him in his personal vehicle because it was against the Granted Wishes Village policy and procedure. Scott didn't care about the rules, but he knew that if something happened to Toby, his mother would sue anyone and everyone. Then, he got an idea.

"Just for the record, my plan did not include you falling out of a tree, but I'm going to fix things. Ok?" Scott asked.

"Ok," Toby replied. The sobbing had turned to whimpering as he lay on the grass. Scott grabbed his radio.

"The king is here! Unit 96. The king is here, over!"

"Everything is going to be ok," Scott said, trying to be reassuring. Seven minutes later, Scott heard the familiar sound of the sirens. Scott left the gate on automatic when he left, so he stayed with Toby until the ambulance arrived. JoJo was driving this time, and they got out arguing.

"I can't believe you drove through a back yard!" Perry exclaimed.

"It saved us going through the light at Boggy Creek, didn't it?" JoJo replied.

"But you took out that old woman's clothes line!" Perry said. Scott yelled, "Hey!" at them and waved them over. They pushed the stretcher through the grass to where Toby lay. Perry grabbed the medical bag and unzipped while JoJo lowered the stretcher down.

"I think he broke his arm," Scott said. Not necessarily an emergency, but Scott had a plan. They loaded him on the stretcher, raised it back up, and headed back to the ambulance. Scott pulled Perry aside and briefly explained the situation and the plan he had. Perry agreed and got in the back of the ambulance with Toby, and Scott shut the door and pounded the side twice. JoJo took off towards Kissimmee Regional Medical Center. Scott radioed the office and explained to Marie that he had to go to the hospital because he didn't want to leave Toby by himself. Marie was very familiar with Jessica Driskoll by this point of their stay and said she would cover for him. As Scott drove to the hospital, he called Robert Finnell, who was also familiar with Jessica Driskoll.

"Yeah, Kissimmee Regional. I'm headed there now. And could you contact Frank Goodman in Stuart? He needs to be involved," Scott asked his friend. He finally made it to the hospital and walked into the emergency room. He found a nurse who led him to Toby. He was in a bed sectioned off by curtains in the emergency room.

"How are you doing, bud?" Scott asked.

"I'm ok. It hurt when they took blood, though," Toby replied. Granted Wishes Village had several pages of medical release forms that every family had to sign in case of an emergency. The board never thought about an event happening that a parent wouldn't be there for, but the legal department did. So, to cover any future liability, any minor staying at Granted Wishes Village could receive medical care without a parent or guardian present. And families had to submit full medical records of their child's condition. Jessica Driskoll got a doctor she was buying pills from to fabricate the documents for her.

"Everything is going to be alright," Scott said as he patted his leg. He was nervous that this was going to fall apart in his lap, but Scott Cooper was intent on doing the right thing. At least what he thought was the right thing. *Am I doing the right thing?* When Robert Finnell walked into the emergency room, he felt a lot better. He was dressed in slacks, a button-down shirt, and a non-descript tie. Osceola County Sheriff's Department had some leniency on their detectives, so Robert didn't have to wear a jacket in summer time. But he did have his gun holstered under his arm and a badge on his belt. He saw Scott and walked over. They shook hands, and Scott introduced Robert to Toby.

"You must be Toby. I've heard a lot about you," Robert said. Toby's right arm was in a sling, so they fist bumped with their left hands.

"Were you able to contact Mr. Goodman?" Scott asked.

"You found my dad?!" Toby asked excitedly. He started to get up, but Scott stopped him and had him lay back down with his head on the pillow.

"He's on his way," Robert replied. This caused Toby to smile. Scott's phone buzzed, and he pulled it out to read the text. It was from Marie telling Scott that Jessica Driskoll was on her way. *This might just come together.* 20 minutes later, Jessica Driskoll stormed into the emergency room and started yelling, "Where's my baby?!" over and over again. She wore a white tank top that was a size too small, which caused her boobs to hang out. She spotted Toby and ran over to him. She threw her arms around his head and turned to Scott.

"What did you do to my baby?" she barked at him.

"He fell out of a tree behind your cottage," Scott replied. She looked over and saw Robert Finnell on the other side of the bed and noticed the badge.

"Well, that's impossible. He has leukemia and has to be in a wheelchair," she said nervously. Just then, the attending E.R. physician approached the bed, holding a chart.

Dr. Vashal Padilla graduated the top of his class from the University of New Delhi. He was shorter than average height and wore round glasses and he was in his third year at Kissimmee Regional Medical Center and truly loved his job. The E.M.T. that brought Toby Driskoll in talked with Dr. Padilla before he left and the battery of tests he did concluded what was told to him. He walked over to bed 21 to see a detective, a security guard, and a portly woman standing around the bed of a boy. *This should be interesting*, Dr. Padilla thought.

"Mr. Driskoll, my name is Dr. Padilla. How are you feeling?" he asked. He was looking right at Toby and ignoring everyone else standing around the bed.

"I'm ok. My arm hurts, though," Toby replied.

"Well, I've seen your x-rays, and you have a hairline fracture in the right humerus. Not too funny, is it?" Dr. Padilla joked. Scott chuckled. It's the kind of joke his dad would make. "But, you're not dying of that or anything else. As far as I can see, you are a healthy young man that should lay off the sugary sodas." Jessica Driskoll tried to look shocked. Then she ran over to him and tried to give him a hug. "You've cured him!" Dr. Padilla put up the chart to shield him from the advancing harlot.

"Ms. Driskoll, my name is Detective Robert Finnell. I have some questions I'd like to ask you down at the station," he said. He pulled some hand cuffs out of his pocket and made his way towards her.

"What?! Wait! I didn't do anything! Hang on!" She was backing up towards the door. Robert grabbed her right arm and pulled it behind her back. He then grabbed the other and cuffed them together. Scott pulled the curtains closed, so Toby didn't have to see his mother getting read her rights. Dr. Padilla cleared his throat and returned to being a doctor.

"So, it doesn't require a cast, just this sling for the next six to eight weeks. I suggest low dosage ibuprofen for the pain, but otherwise he's good to go," Dr. Padilla explained, now facing Scott.

"Thanks, Doc," Scott said, and Dr. Padilla pulled open the curtain and left. Scott looked down at Toby. He expected him to be unhinged over seeing his mother arrested, but he laid there like he was watching television.

"It's ok. This wasn't the first time," Toby said. Scott laughed and lightly punched him in the leg. An hour and a half later, Frank Goodman arrived and ran towards his boy. He put his arms around him and kissed him on the head. He was a tan man, about Scott's age, and smelled like bait. He was the first mate aboard the *Lady Stuart*, an 80-foot day boat that would take anglers out five miles into the Gulf Stream and fish for snapper and grouper off the many reefs. When Scott saw his cap with the *Lady Stuart* name on it, he was reminded of the many times he and his friends would wait in the river for it to return, so they could jump the wake in their boats. It was a successful jump if you could hear the whine of the propeller leaving the water as the boat went airborne.

"Are you alright? I've missed you so much! Have you been getting my letters? I send one every week. Tell me what happened. I can't wait…" Frank Goodman was gushing over his son. Scott let the two of them talk and catch up. He was about to leave when Frank Goodman turned around.

"Are you Scott Cooper? The man the detective told me about?" he asked.

"Yes, I am."

"Thank you so much for taking care of my son. I really appreciate it." Scott looked at him, and with the exception of the hair and eyes, Toby looked exactly like his father. Scott reached his hand out, but Frank hugged him and patted him repeatedly on the back, leaving behind the smell of fish guts that now permeated the air. He went back to Toby, who waved Scott over.

"Thank you for helping me with my wish," Toby said. He held out his left hand and made a fist, and Scott gave him a bump.

"No problem," Scott said. He left the emergency room and walked to his car, feeling good about himself. On the way back to Granted Wishes

Village, he thought about the way Frank Goodman interacted with Toby, and it reminded him of his relationship with Carl. Scott was glad he made the decision on the dock to stand up and do something. *Now there is one last loose end to tie up.*

〖 X X I 〗

Robert Finnell pulled his undercover police car into Scott Cooper's apartment complex and waited for Scott. Tonight was the night they were hopefully going to catch someone trying to dump waste into the lake. Scott came out dressed as much like Skeet as his wardrobe would allow. He was dressed in boots, blue jeans, a t-shirt from the Daytona 500, and a baseball cap.

"Well, you sure nailed the 'white trash' look," Robert joked.

"Shut up!" Scott fired back. "I had to borrow the shirt from a neighbor." Robert pulled his Impala out and onto Narcoossee Road and headed north. They got stuck behind a slow driving mini-van, and Scott turned to his friend of many years.

"Hey, remember that time I came up with the idea to put in a wine cooler system in your Llama van?" Scott asked, knowing it was going to bring a debate.

"I came up with the idea!" Robert shot back. The summer of their junior year, they were out driving around Stuart in the mini-van that was handed down to Robert. It was the family van that had been his older brother and older sister's first car, and now it was his. It was Scott that pointed out the fact that there were windshield wipers for the front and back on this particular make and model. He then theorized that there was a separate windshield washer fluid container for the front and the back. It was Robert that took the idea and ran with it. They quickly drove to Home Depot and purchased several feet of tubing and two small copper valves. They drove back to Robert's house because his mom was gone for the afternoon. After draining the back-windshield container and rinsing it out twice, Robert hooked up the rubber hose and then put a T-junction. He then attached two rubber hoses to the two ends of the T-junction. Scott helped him run the rubber tubing under the plastic molding that ran the inside length of the mini-van. On the left and right side of the front seat, right above the seat belts, Robert drilled holes in the molding and mounted the copper valves. They attached the rubber tubing to the valves and then cut two smaller tubes as straws and twisted them on. The idea was to fill the back-windshield container with wine coolers, and then while you were driving, simply turn on the windshield wash, and the pump would push wine cooler through the tubes and into their mouths. Robert even wrapped the rubber tubing around an air conditioner coil, so the wine coolers would be nice and cold. What they had not counted on was the pounds per square the liquid would shoot out of the rubber straws, which equated to a garden hose wide open. On the maiden voyage, it was a bright and sunny day. So, it was rather suspicious to see a mini-van with two teenage boys driving down A1A with the windshield wipers flinging back and forth and rubber tubes hanging from the ceiling. When Robert turned on the windshield wipers and hit the "wash" button, the wine coolers shot into their mouths with so much force, Scott threw up all over the dash. He took the hose out of his mouth, which caused it to spray all over him. Robert spit a mouthful of wine cooler into his lap, and the hose fell into his right shirt pocket. Robert finally turned the "wash" feature off in time to verve back onto the road they were driving on.

They were pulled over, and when the police officer saw the inside of the van with two teenage boys soaking wet and vomit on the dash board and tubes hanging from the ceiling, dripping, he shook his head and walked back to his car and drove off. Unfortunately, the wine cooler express system did not add any extra value to the mini-van upon trade in.

"Yeah, when my mom asked about it, I told her it was in the event of loss of cabin pressure," Robert replied, and they both laughed. They got quiet, so Robert turned on the radio. Scott stared straight ahead as Robert drove them to the fish camp. "Us and Them," by Pink Floyd was playing.

"You sure you want to go through with this? I can always get a deputy to do it," Robert asked his friend. He could tell Scott was getting nervous.

"No, I'm good. I want to do this," Scott said. He was getting nervous because Tori had told him that the Russian, Crazy Yaz, carried a gun. Robert Finnell stopped at the gate and let Scott out. The gate had been unlocked since Skeet kidnapped Tori, so all he had to do was remove the chain and let Robert through. He watched Robert drive down the dirt road, and he closed the gate and waited for the Russian.

Crazy Yaz turned right at the curve and headed for gate. He was right on time and wanted to get this over with quickly because this was his least favorite job. Ed Turnbull had been on another one of his week-long benders and left him in charge of the operations. No one had seen or heard from the two guys out at the lake, so he hoped they would be there. *I better not have to deal with this by myself.* He pulled up and watched the gate open. *Hmmm, usually it's the big guy opening the gate,* Crazy Yaz thought to himself. He drove down the dirt road and arrived at the fish camp. He didn't see the big guy and started to get nervous. He turned the truck and started backing down the boat ramp when head lights appeared from behind a cabin with a strobing blue light on the dash.

"Stop the truck and get out with your hands up!" Robert Finnell yelled into the megaphone. Crazy Yaz panicked. He reached for his .38 when he heard the sirens and saw the blue lights of a couple of police cars speeding up the dirt road towards him. When he looked back, there was a man with a large nose and dark hair pointing a gun at him. "I said get out with your hands up!"

Robert Finnell arrested Crazy Yaz for conspiracy to commit illegal dumping and possession of a stolen fire arm. He put the handcuffed Russian into the back of a squad car and watched the two deputies pull out. He looked at Scott and smiled.

"Well done, my friend. Now comes the dull and not so glorious part of police work. We have to wait here for a tow truck and being 12:30 at night in the middle of nowhere, that could take a while," Robert said.

"I'll take it back," Scott replied.

"You sure?"

"Yeah, Tori can pick me up. She's getting off soon. Just call ahead and let the impound lot know I'm coming."

"Ok, if you say so." Scott climbed into the pump truck and started it up. His dad taught him how to drive stick on an old pick-up truck on his grandfather's farm. This was quite a bit bigger, but the principles were the same. He stalled putting it into first two times, but it all came back to him. He slowly made his way down the dirt road, passed the gate, and onto East Parkway. When he got to Narcoossee Road, he made a left and started his way to Kissimmee to drop the pump truck off at the police impound lot. Before he got to County Road 530, he passed Great Pine Pass, the road Ed Turnbull lived on. Scott turned the pump truck around and made a right. He didn't know where exactly he lived, but there was only one bright red, 2001 Ford F-150 King cab in the whole town. He found the truck parked in the driveway of a large house. Scott drove the pump truck down the block and parked. He snuck through the front yard of the house next to his and followed a hedge of hibiscus to the back yard. He crept around and found the pool area. The lights were on in the pool, and the Jacuzzi was still bubbling, and steaming. Passed out on a lounge chair was the same man he saw that night at the Pirate's Booty. Except now, he was wearing only speedos. An empty bottle of Jack Daniels was in one hand and what appeared to be panties were in the other. There was a trail of clothes that led to the sliding glass door to the back bedroom. Once he saw the boots, Scott knew Ed had beguiled some cocktail waitress from his club over. Ed was snoring loud enough for Scott to hear 20-feet away, so he felt it was safe to pull off Operation Karma.

Scott Cooper pulled the truck up Ed Turnbull's driveway. He stopped ten-feet shy of the F-150. He got out and took the hose off the side and hooked it up to the back of the tank. He climbed into the bed of the truck when he noticed the back window. It looked like someone had pried it open, so Scott opened the window and lowered the hose into the cab. He went back and turned the valve. The cabin filled up in no time. He turned the valve back and pulled the hose into the truck bed. He turned the valve again and watched raw sewage fill Ed Turnbull's truck. It couldn't possibly equate to all the damage Ed did to the many lakes in the area over the years, but it did make Scott feel a little better. He unhooked the hose and put it back on the side. He got into the pump truck, pulled around the circular drive-way, and drove away with the head lights off. When he got to the end of the street, he turned his lights on and headed back out to Narcoossee Road.

Scott made it to the impound lot and turned the truck over to the night officer. He signed some papers and made his way back to the street. After 15 minutes, he saw Tori turn the corner in his Cavalier. She pulled up, stopped, and opened the door.

"Why'd you bring my car instead of the Mustang?" he asked.

"You're not riding in my baby tainted!" she replied.

After processing, Robert Finnell took Yazoff Klebnikov to a briefing room and asked him several questions about why he was in possession of a septic truck and what he was doing at an abandoned fish camp at midnight. Yazoff Klebnikov just drank coffee and chain smoked cigarettes. Finally, after 15 minutes, Robert realized that he wasn't going to talk, so he got up to leave when Crazy Yaz finally spoke.

"Phone call," was all he said. Robert Finnell picked up the receiver of the phone on the table.

"I'm assuming it's long distance?" Crazy Yaz nodded, and Robert Finnell pressed 9 and handed the phone to him. He dialed the number of a cell phone store in Newark, New Jersey and put the headset to his ear.

"Da," the voice on the other end said.

"Vybrostie menya k cherty ot/suda!" was what he yelled into the phone, which in Russian translates to, "Get me the hell out of here!"

At eight am the following morning, Robert Finnell rang the doorbell to the Turnbull residence. He waited, and no one answered. He rang the bell again and knocked. From behind the door, a muffled, "who's there?" came out. Robert took his badge and held it to the peephole and replied, "Detective Robert Finnell with the Osceola County Sheriff's Department. I'd like to ask you some questions." There was a fumbling of locks, and the door opened. Behind the door was a sight to be seen. A large man with blond hair and a beer gut stood before Robert. He was in his mid-30's and wore a red speedo and a bath robe. His eyes were the color of a west coast sunset, and he smelled like a distillery. *He probably hasn't seen his feet in years,* Robert thought to himself.

"What seems to be the officer, problem?" Ed slurred and then burped.

"I caught a man trying to illegally dump sewage into East Lake Tohopekaliga. The truck belongs to you. Know anything about this?" Robert asked.

"My truck?" Robert Finnell noted that Ed's face perked up when he mentioned what happened.

"Yes. Your truck. *Sanitation King* painted on the side. License plate number 682-YRK. Registered to one Edward Nelson Turnbull. I'm assuming that's you?"

"Well, I had nothing to do with it. I was here all night with a beautiful young lady. I have been for several days," Ed replied. He was started to sweat along his forehead and his upper lip quivered.

"I arrested a Yazoff Klebnikov. You know him?"

"Never heard of him."

"Would you know why he was in possession of your truck?"

"He probably stole it."

"A sewage truck?"

"Yeah."

"A sewage truck?" Robert asked again.

"Sure. Happens all the time," Ed replied.

"A sewage truck?"

"I knew a guy in Fort Pierce who had three stolen in one night. Bunch of teenagers joyriding. Made a God-awful mess of the You Pick 'Em Field."

"Sewage... trucks?" Robert Finnell was always amazed at the stories people would tell to proclaim their innocence. Nine times out of ten, they started with, "so, what happened wuz..." There was the man Robert pulled over for speeding that led to a failed sobriety test. When asked why he was speeding drunk, the man replied, "If I drive faster, I get to my destination quicker, thus minimizing loss of life." When Robert was still a rookie deputy, he got a call for a carjacking. He found the car and hit the lights, which caused the driver of the stolen vehicle to panic and speed off. Robert followed him into an apartment complex where he crashed the car and ran into an apartment. Robert followed him in and searched the entire place and couldn't find him. The windows were boarded up in the back, and there was only one way in, the front door. The place was empty, and he couldn't for the life of him figure out how the man escaped. He sat on the couch and waited for his back-up when he heard a hmph! come out. Robert got up and pulled the cushions off and didn't see anything. He then turned the couch over, and the man had crawled up underneath the couch and was hiding inside. When Robert asked what he was doing in there, his reply was, "resting." But this one was going to be his new favorite with the boys down at the station. Stolen septic truck.

"This Yazzy fella, I want him prosecuted to the fullest extent of the law!" Ed demanded. A breeze blew in, and Ed Turnbull threw up a little in his mouth as he caught whiff of the shit stew the morning sunshine was cooking up. He pushed the detective out of the way and made his way to his beloved pick-up truck.

"What the-" was all he could get out before he vomited all over his slippers. *It's possible the Russian came over here before the fish camp, but this has Scott written all over it.* Robert smiled. When Ed Turnbull finished vomiting, he wiped his mouth with the sleeve of his bath robe and stood upright.

"You tell that sum' bitch he's messed with the wrong big dog!" Ed Turnbull yelled at the detective as he stormed his way into the house and slammed the door. *I guess this interview is concluded.*

Ed Turnbull knew the ramifications of imprisoning the nephew of a Russian crime boss, but it wasn't like he could bail him out of jail without looking guilty. Ed also knew that with his one phone, Crazy Yaz probably called his uncle in New Jersey to update him on his current situation. Which meant two things to Ed Turnbull: One, Crazy Yaz would be out of jail soon. Two, it meant that as of this morning, there was a hit out for him. That meant he only had a couple of hours to get the hell out of Dodge. It was in that moment he decided that now would be a great time to take a much-needed vacation. *A tropical destination would be a nice change of pace to lay low for a few weeks while all this blows over*, he thought. Ed Turnbull walked into his kitchen and rinsed his mouth out with water. He put a pot of coffee on to sober up from the night. And then turned on his computer, and while it was booting up, he hastily started packing a suitcase. His companion was in the shower, and Ed felt he had enough time for a quickie before he planned his escape. He thought about taking her with him, but he dismissed the idea when he calculated the cost. While he was toweling off, he suggested she go home and take the day off. Afterwards, he then went to the kitchen, poured a cup of coffee, and sat down at his computer. He started looking for sunny destinations to hide from the Russian mob.

XXII

Scott went to work the next day, tired from the night before. He had been through a lot these past couple of weeks. More than he ever had his entire 35 years. Normally, he hated being out of his boring routine, but now he was embracing it. He felt alive again. When Scott finished the morning check-in, his friend Henry Weisel pulled up, in uniform.

"Hey, Henry. What are you doing here?" Scott asked.

"I don't know. They called me up first thing this morning and told me to come in," Henry replied. And in an instant, that "alive" feeling was replaced with worry and uneasiness.

"Oh, ok," Scott said, deflated. Henry looked at Scott and then looked into his lap and shook his head. They both knew what this meant, but it was a crappy way to find out. Scott took a deep breath and let it out. Marie called him on the radio, except she wasn't so pleasant sounding this time.

"Scott? Mr. Kawalski needs to see you in his office." It was the first time she called him by his first name and not Officer Friendly. He walked to the

Administration building and looked over at Pete Possum. *It doesn't look like my wish to keep my job will be granted today, Mr. Possum.*

Scott sat down in the very chair he did three months ago when he first started his job. Lenny Kawalski shut the door behind him and sat down behind his desk and looked at Scott like a man who had bad news to give.

"That was one hell of a tackle you did on that guy," Scott said to break the ice.

"Yeah, I guess it was," Lenny said. "So, listen, sport. I gotta let you go. The board agreed that all this craziness didn't happen before you got here, and the common denominator is you. There was one lone dissenting vote from an anonymous board member, and I fought like hell to get you to stay. But in the end, the 'ayes' had it. Sorry, sport," Lenny said. He looked genuinely upset.

"Well, that's ok, Mr. Kawalski. I was the world's worst security guard," Scott said.

"Second worst. The guy you replaced fell asleep behind the wheel of the Officer Friendly mobile and drove it into the pond. We had to get a tow truck out here to fish it out!" Lenny said, and both men let out a laugh. "Go ahead and give me your radio and keys. You can keep the badge."

"When did you notice it said 'Galaxy Patrol?'" Scott asked as his cheeks turned red out of embarrassment.

"The first day. But I figured if you can patrol the galaxy, you could patrol this place," Lenny replied, and that brought more laughing.

"Do you mind if I say good-bye to some people and gather my things?" Scott asked.

"Sure, sport. Good luck to you." Lenny Kawalski stood up and extended his hand, and the two men shook hands. And just like before, Lenny gripped him like a dock worker. "Go Badgers!"

"Go Badgers!" Scott shot back. He was a Seminole at heart, but he was willing to make an exception in this case. He left Lenny's office and walked down the hall towards the back door when a woman emerged from the restroom. She was drying her hands with a paper towel as she came out and looked startled but then recognized him and smiled.

"Oh, there you are." It was the crazy old woman that sped by him every morning.

"It's you!" Scott had to admit that up close, she was very attractive for her age. Her hair was auburn and grey, and she had a cute button nose. "Why are you in such a hurry every day?"

"Oh, that. I like the pancake station, and if I don't beat Gloria, she gets it, and I'm stuck on eggs. And I don't like eggs." she replied. "I'm sorry about what happened. I did try for you to keep your job."

"I guess the weight of a cafeteria worker doesn't pull like it used to," Scott said sarcastically.

"Funny," she replied and gave him a look like a grandmother about to scold you for leaving the milk out. "Anyways, I want you to know that I appreciate all that you've done here," she said. She opened her purse and pulled out a folded piece of paper. "This is for you." Scott opened the paper up, and it was a check for $10,000. Signed, Lillian Stultzman.

"Wait, you're the founder of Granted Wishes Villages?"

"Ding, ding, ding! We have a winner!" she said and smiled. *Tori says that all the time, what the hell?* Scott looked at the portrait of Lillian Stultzman hanging on the wall behind her, and it looked nothing like the woman standing in front of him.

"Who's that?" Scott pointed to the painting.

"That's Ethel. We play bridge together on Fridays. I didn't want anyone to know who I was, so I made sure the board changed right after I left, so I wouldn't be recognized. I like to come in and volunteer a few days a week and keep an eye on things. And I just love the kids. Anyways, I still have a vote on the board, but I don't have to attend all those boring meetings. And I use my maiden name here, Lisicki."

✳

Scott was still in shock when he reached the movie theater. He walked down the aisle and made his way to the changing room. All the characters were there, including Tori. She was in her full princess costume, and she looked simply stunning. Tori got up and ran to Scott and gave him a big hug.

"I'm so sorry. Aunt Lilly told me last night but made me promise not to say anything," Tori told him.

"She was the relative that got you the job here, right?"

"Ding, ding, ding! We have a winner!" Tori said and smiled.

"Well, at least I know where you got that from," he said and went in to kiss her. She stopped him with her one finger.

"Later, I've got make-up on." She smiled and flashed those beautiful green eyes. He said his good-byes to the alligator and the bear. King Leopold bowed regally.

"You're right. It does come off better in costume," Scott said, and both men laughed and shook hands. He turned back to Tori.

"My house later?" Scott asked. "I'm making blackened shrimp and grits!"

"Oh, you do know your way to a girl's heart!" she said in a southern drawl.

Scott walked to the maintenance garage to say good-bye to Mr. Lucas. They had an odd relationship, but Scott really liked the guy, and he was going to miss him and their little talks. When he got there, a round, white man wearing a blue shirt with *Walter* stitched on the pocket greeted him.

"Can I help you?" he asked.

"I was looking for Mr. Lucas. I wanted to say good-bye," Scott replied.

"Mr. Lucas? No one here by that name," Walter said. He took a handkerchief out of his back pocket and started cleaning his glasses.

"You sure? Older black man? Mustache? Salt and pepper hair?"

"I've worked day shift here for the last five years, and the night crew is all Latino. No Mr. Lucas. Sorry." Walter put his glasses on and walked over to the desk and started tinkering with something. Scott left, feeling confused.

I know I didn't imagine him. Scott walked to Granted Wishes Circle and started back to the guard shack when he saw Mr. Lucas walking in the opposite direction.

"Mr. Lucas! Mr. Lucas!" Scott yelled as he ran towards him. Mr. Lucas stopped walking and turned around. He smiled at Scott and waved.

"Mr. Lucas, I'm so glad I found you. I wanted to say good-bye. I got let go today," Scott said, breathing heavy.

"Yeah, I heard about that. Sorry, son. But remember, when God shuts one door, he always opens another," Mr. Lucas replied.

"So, Walt at the maintenance garage said you don't work here. Are you finally going to tell me what you do here?" Scott asked.

"I will, but first, answer me this: did you become the man you wanted your son to grow up to be?"

"Yeah, I think I did," he paused. "Wait a minute, how do you know about that? I don't remember mentioning that to you."

"And do you still think you're too small or insignificant to be used by God? Didn't you help reunite a son with his father? Stop an evil man from poisoning our lakes? Indirectly got rid of two dangerous men?"

"Yeah, I guess I did," Scott said. He hadn't really thought of it that way.

"Sounds to me like you took a stand and became a man. And fulfilled what you decided on the dock with Toby Driskoll," Mr. Lucas said. He looked at his watch. "It's almost time. You want to see what I do here, son?" Mr. Lucas started walking on the sidewalk towards the cottages.

"Yes. Please. Don't keep me in suspense any longer," Scott said half sarcastically.

"When you get home, look up Matthew 18:10. It'll put things into perspective," Mr. Lucas said. And everything stopped. Scott couldn't move. He could look around with his eyes but not move his head. He looked up and saw a blue jay in midflight. He looked down and saw water from a sprinkler frozen in time. It was like he was looking at a picture, but Mr.

Lucas kept moving. And he was different now. Ghost-like and ethereal. Scott could see him walking towards a cottage, but he could also see right through him. And his clothes changed. The blue shirt with his name stitched in, and his dark blue work pants were replaced with a long white robe. Mr. Lucas walked through the door and into the cottage. He returned later walking and holding the hand of a little girl. She too was ghost-like and ethereal. And a bright light appeared opposite of them. It was like a tunnel of light started in the pine forest and gradually got bigger and opened right in front of the cottage. The only sound Scott could hear was Mr. Lucas' voice.

"Everything is fine, Stacy. I'm going to take you to someone that is really excited to meet you. He's told me all about you. He's going to take you someplace where you will never hurt or be sick again. Someplace where there are no more tears. It's a place of great rejoicing. And you'll see your family again." The little girl looked up at Mr. Lucas and smiled. They walked hand in hand towards the light. The light was so bright, Scott couldn't look at it directly, but he could make someone out. There was a figure standing in the cone of light. He couldn't see his face, but he could definitely see arms reaching out. The figure in the light hugged the little girl and bent down on one knee. He was talking with her, but Scott couldn't hear what was being said. The little girl hugged the figure in the light again. And just like that, the light, Mr. Lucas, and the little girl disappeared. And then someone pressed play. The bird flew overhead, and the sprinkler water rained down. Scott continued his next step like he was un-paused. In the distance, he heard a radio blare, "The king is here! The king is here! Unit 45! The king is here!" Scott looked over at the cottage Mr. Lucas just came out of. 45.

Later that night, Scott told the story of Mr. Lucas to Tori over dinner and remembered the verse. He grabbed his Bible off the shelf and turned to Matthew. "See that you do not look down on one of these little ones. For I tell you that their angels in heaven always see the face of my Father in heaven."

XXIII

The Choctaw Indian tribe of southern Mississippi has a legend about an alligator that helped them become the greatest deer hunters in history that hunted responsibly and with respect for their brother animals. Deep in the marshy forest near the Gulf of Mexico, a Choctaw man was out hunting, quite unsuccessfully. He would find a deer and aim his bow and arrow, but a bird would cry out and startle the deer. Or he would get close to a deer and snap a twig, causing the deer to run away. He would miss high and low. And he would come back empty handed each time. One day, the Choctaw man walked deep into the swamp and vowed not to return until he had a deer. After several days, he still had not caught a deer. He was looking around when he came upon a dry pit where there had once been water. There, at the bottom, lay an alligator. He hadn't had water for days and was on the verge of death. The man looked at the pitiful creature and said, "Brother alligator, your luck is worse than mine."

"I must find water, but I am too weak to travel. I know that you try and try, but the deer always escapes your arrow. Take me to water, and I will teach you to be a great deer hunter," the alligator said in a weak voice.

"May I tie your legs together and your mouth shut?" the man asked.

"Yes," the alligator said, and it rolled on its back. He used his belt to tie the alligator's mouth shut and some vines to tie the legs. He put the alligator on his shoulders and walked through the swamp. After many hours, he found a deep pool of water and untied the alligator.

"Thank you," he said. "Now do as I say, and you will become a great hunter. Go into the forest with your bow and arrows. First, you will meet a sister doe. She will be small. She is too young, so you must not shoot her. Greet her and move on. Next, you will meet a larger sister doe," the alligator continued. "She is a mother with fawns. She will have fawns each year for many years, so you must not shoot her. Greet her and move on." The man nodded.

"Next, you will meet a brother buck. He will not be very large. He is young and will father many fawns, so you must not shoot him. Greet him and move on." The man was puzzled, but he agreed to follow the alligator's instructions.

"Finally, you will meet a larger brother buck. He will be tall and old. He has had a long life and will be ready to give it to you, so you may shoot him. Or," the alligator said," he is too fat, dumb, and stupid to know that he is in danger. In that case, remove him from the herd."

The hunter did as the alligator instructed, and he shot his first deer. He triumphantly brought the deer home to the rest of the tribe. And over the feast that night, the hunter shared the story of the wise alligator in the pit to his tribe. And that's how the Choctaw Indian tribe of southern Mississippi became the best deer hunters of any tribe in the land.

XXIV

Nikolai Dvorchek hung up the phone with his nephew and called out to the back of his cell phone store. A large man with no neck appeared. He looked like a flesh rectangle.

"Get me the Fixer," he said to the man with no neck. He returned to the back of the store and looked up a number in an old rolodex. He picked up the phone on the wall and dialed the number. No one knew his real name or anything about him, but the Russian mob knew he "fixed" things. There was never an assignment he didn't complete, but he did have one rule: no children. His fee was quite large but justifiable because of his success rate. Normally, the mob liked to take care of things themselves, but his nephew was his sister's kid. And he would never hear the end of it if something happened to Yaz. And it was him who sent his nephew down to Florida in the first place, which puts the responsibility squarely on him. Plus, his sister was married to Nikolai's counterpart in New York, who was always such a prick to him, so Nikolai Dvorchek went with an outside contractor. An hour later, a black Cadillac pulled up and parked outside the cell phone store. A tall man got out and entered the store. He wore an all-black Armani suit and dark sunglasses. His dark hair was brushed back, and he had tan skin. No one knew if he was Italian or Hispanic or even eastern European. He looked like everyone and no one at the same time. But two things stood out about him. One was his height. He was six-foot, three inches. The other, on his right hand, there was a tattoo of a large skull atop a mountain with several little skulls surrounding the large skull. Some-one asked him what the skulls represented and why on his right hand, and the Fixer replied his right hand had done a lot of bad things, and each skull was a man he killed. Currently, there were 32.

"What can I do for you, Mr. Dvorchek?" the Fixer asked.

"My nephew is in some shit-hole jail in Florida. And he is important. I need you to go get him out and bring him here to me. Also, I need you to teach a very fat, stupid man a lesson. Use extreme prejudice. Here's the in-formation," Nikolai Dvorchek explained. He took out a piece of paper from his shirt pocket and handed it to the Fixer. Then, he pulled out a thick en-velope of cash out of the register and slid it across the display case.

"Any particular way?" the Fixer asked.

"Be creative," Nikolai Dvorchek answered and smiled. He watched the Fixer leave the store and enter his car. He drove away, and Nikolai Dvorchek forgot about the matter, that's how good he was. What no one knew was the Fixer was a former Mossad agent. He was born and raised in Tel Aviv, Israel, and when he graduated high school, there was mandatory military service for two years. He did his time and decided to stay in the Israeli army. He was an outstanding soldier, and he was selected from his squad for con-sideration for the *HaMossad leModi'in ule Tafkidim Meyuhadim,* or the Mossad, which means in Hebrew, "Institute for Intelligence and Special Opera-tions." It is the Israeli intelligence agency that is in charge of intelligence gathering, covert operations, and counter-terrorism. The Director of the Mossad answers directly to the Prime Minister. And unlike the government and the military, the Mossad is exempt from the laws of Israel. David Gottlieb, A.K.A. the Fixer, spent eight years in the military and another ten as an agent in the Mossad. After his mother passed away, he left the agency and Israel and moved to America to freelance. His skill set was always in demand because he was, by definition, a professional. Most of the muscle used on the street level was just big guys with guns. There were several ex-*KGB* agents, but they were usually higher up doing security for the big bosses. The Fixer, on the other hand, knew how to work with explosives, poison someone, and make it look like an accident, shoot a target over a mile away, etc. The stuff the Russians had him do was child's play considering he spent 72 hours hiding on a roof in Syria, waiting to shoot an Iranian general with a high-powered rifle.

Hubba's Grub and Subs was the morning gathering place for the town of Narcoossee. It's where everyone came by to swap gossip and trade fishing secrets and hot spots. There was a long counter that had 15 stools and several tables along the windows. People had their regular tables and their regular waitresses. The cook would look through the window and see the same 50 faces, week after week, and knew their order from beginning to end. Just like every morning at this time, the place was packed. Every stool at the counter had a person on it, and all the tables were full. But today was different because Mack Quinn was there. He was an older man with a full head of grey hair and had bright, rosy cheeks. He was the lone barber in the area, so he was well-known to the community. In a town as small as Narcoossee, everyone knew everyone else. So, everyone there knew he had three daughters, the youngest, Marie, worked at Granted Wishes Village. Mack Quinn took a bite of his biscuit and told the restaurant what his daughter had been telling him the last couple of weeks. The smell of freshly brewed coffee filled the air as everyone ate their breakfast and quietly listened to the adventures of the world's second worst security guard. Mack Quinn began with the story of Jessica Driskoll and Toby and how Scott got the boy to his daddy. He told them about Skeet and Tahoe at the fish camp and Tahoe's demise at the jaws of Lucille, the three-legged alligator. He explained how Skeet chased Scott Cooper and Tori in the movie theater and brought up Lenny Kawalski's tackle. Just then, a man seated next to Mack Quinn stood up and addressed the patrons.

"I just got off my shift, and I'm here to tell you Scott Cooper helped stop a man from dumping sewage into East Lake Toho."

Everyone gasped in unbelief that someone would pollute the lake that everyone there had swum, fished, or boated on at one point in their life. People started murmuring to one another in hushed voices. Everyone in the restaurant knew who owned the truck. *The Sanitation King.* Ed Turnbull. And the man who spoke up turned out to be the deputy who drove Crazy Yaz to jail.

"Yeah, what makes me madder than a horned toad is they're firing him as we speak. Marie knew when she left on Monday because she had to run an ad for his replacement," Mack Quinn said. That got the restaurant customers fired up, and the murmuring grew to yelling.

Patrick Smythe sat at the end of the counter and watched the restaurant stir into a frenzy when his cell phone rang.

"Yup," he answered. He listened for a minute. "Ok, get dressed up and check out his house," he said and hung up the phone. He stood up and addressed the restaurant. He had clout in the community because he was the great grandson of G.B. Smythe, one of the original settlers of Narcoossee. He grew up listening to the tale of the betrayal of the Turnbulls from his father, who told him the tale from his father, starting with G.B. Smythe. When he was younger, he couldn't understand how he was to hate a family because of something their great-grandfather did, but just like hating someone because of their race, it was taught to him. When Ed Turnbull moved to town, and rumors started to circulate about his shady septic removal business, Patrick Smythe felt ashamed for not knowing better. He had the proof that he needed that his father was right all along. There was no good in Ed Turnbull. None, what so ever. And now he was going to come to judgement. Patrick Smythe hung up the phone and looked at his zippo lighter. It was given to him by his troop when he was promoted to Captain in the Civil War re-enactment, and that gave him an idea.

"Everyone, listen up! Nathan was gassing up at the 7-11 and talked with Jenny behind the counter. She told him that a tall man in a black suit came by and got gas. She also said she thought she saw that Russian that hangs out with Ed Turnbull sitting in the front seat. I think their coming to get Ed. And the Russian probably wants Coop for getting him arrested. I say we help them and rid the town, once and for all, of those men. Who's with me?!" The restaurant exploded with applause and cheers.

"Company A 6th Florida Regiment! Get your uniforms and meet me at Granted Wishes Village!"

Sophia Casidilla worked in the kitchen at Hubba's Grub and Subs. She worked hard and kept to herself, and she was peeling potatoes behind the counter when the entire restaurant paid their tabs and rushed out. She spoke enough English to know what was going on, so she went to the phone that hung on the wall and called her husband, Jose, the head cook at Gordy's Taco Shop.

Ray Huffman stacked the empty glasses on a tray and wiped the table with a wet rag he had in his front apron. He, too, was interested in the story being told in the restaurant. When the guy at the end of the counter started talking about getting Ed Turnbull and the whole restaurant got behind him, Ray knew what he had to do. He walked passed Sophia Casidilla into the kitchen and pulled out his cell phone. He placed a call to his part-time night job at the Pirate's Booty.

"Lil Bit? This is Ray. You're never gonna believe this, but…"

United Airlines flight 762 landed at Orlando International Airport at six the following morning of Crazy Yaz's phone call to his uncle. The Fixer disembarked with the rest of the passengers and walked up the ramp and through the terminal to car rentals. He didn't have any luggage other than a small bag he carried on the plane, so he avoided the chaos of all the tourists. He went straight to Sunrise Rent-a-Car and walked up to the desk. A young woman greeted him and asked for his identification for the rental. She typed on the keyboard and looked at her computer screen and frowned.

"I'm sorry, but we don't have any black Cadillacs available. In that color or any other, I'm afraid. But I do have a black Lincoln Town car. It has the same leg room and gets better-" the Fixer cut her off with his hand and pulled out a fake driver license and a fake credit card with the same name on it with the other and handed them to her. She took them and looked at the driver's license.

"Uh, Igor Myslisha… how do you pronounce your last name?" the rental agent asked as she stared intently at the last name that was a string of consonants.

"Just like it's spelled, honey," he replied and took the fake driver's license out of her hand and put it back into his wallet. While she was in the back retrieving the copies he had to sign, the Fixer got behind the counter and got on the internet and looked up the location of the jail in Osceola County. He found the information he was looking for, exited out of the page he was on, and returned to his original position in front of the counter.

"Here you go, Mr. huh, Mr. Igor," the rental agent said as she handed over the keys. He walked out into the parking lot and found the black Lincoln Town car and opened the door. *At least it's new,* the Fixer thought to himself. He started the car and started the air conditioning. He then called the bails bond man that Nikolai Dvorchek told him to contact and got Crazy Yaz bonded out of jail and released a few hours later. He had orders for the fat business man, but Crazy Yaz kept going on about some rent-a-cop at some resort for sick kids, so he obliged and drove to the resort. That's when the Fixer noticed he was low on gas and pulled into a 7-11.

Scott Cooper was in the guard shack gathering his things. This was a short-lived job for Scott, but he had learned so much in the three months he had been at Granted Wishes Village. He put his journal into his backpack and was about to start walking back to the parking lot when a black

Lincoln Town car pulled in. *Not your normal rental for a family,* Scott thought to himself. When the door opened and a tall man in a dark suit got out, he realized that this was no tourist. He approached Scott and grabbed him by his shirt. He pushed him inside and against the wall of the guard shack and held him with his forearm to Scott's neck. He could barely breathe, and he tried to push the tall man's arm away, but he wasn't strong enough. The Fixer punched him in the gut with his free hand, causing Scott to cough and gasp for air. Crazy Yaz got out of the passenger's side and walked into the guard shack.

"Remember me?" Crazy Yaz asked the security guard, slowly being chocked to unconsciousness. "You're coming with us. When we get Ed Turnbull, all of us are going to have a little talk in a citrus grove." Just then, a fleet of ten pick-up trucks roared to a stop outside the guard shack. The Fixer looked at Crazy Yaz, who shook his head and shrugged his shoulders.

"You guys looking for Ed Turnbull?!" Patrick Smythe shouted. The Fixer released Scott, and the three of them exited the guard shack. "Company A 6th Florida Regiment at your service!" Men dressed in Confederate greys started piling out of the pick-ups, and they all had their muskets. Another pick-up pulled up, and a lone man got out. He, too, was dressed in Confederate grey.

"He's not at his house! And someone filled his F-150 full of shit!" Nathan proclaimed. All eyes turned to Scott.

"What?" Scott asked. Another fleet of pick-ups pulled up to the entrance of Granted Wishes Village, but they were older models and well-worn. Out of the cabs poured the Mexican migrant workers, all dressed in Union blues.

"We want to help you get Ed Turnbull!" Jose Casidilla shouted. "I told them all about Gordy's Taco Shop." The Mexican Union fired their muskets in the air and started shouting in Spanish. Three more cars pulled up to the crowd, and the staff from the Pirate's Booty got out. They were all in their pirate uniforms from work.

"We're in, too! Last week, Ed Turnbull paid us in tacos!" a bartender dressed in a blue and red striped t-shirt said.

"You don't want to know about the tacos, man," Jose Casidilla commented.

"Ok. This is what we're going to do. There's only three ways out of Narcoossee. Union army, go block Narcoossee Road to the north and check every car." The Mexicans responded with a loud, *"Si!"* and took off.

"Pirates, you block Narcoossee Road to the south and do the same thing," Patrick Smythe said. The pirates let out an "Arrr!" and Lil Bit took out her taser and sparked it twice. Blue electricity shot to the ground, and she got into the back seat of a car and sped away.

"Regiment! Ed Turnbull has a house boat docked at East Toho Marina. My bet is he's gonna try and cross the lake to St. Cloud. To the marina!" Patrick Smythe ordered his men. They piled back into their trucks and took off. Patrick Smythe turned and looked at the Fixer and Crazy Yaz. "Coop rides with me, and you boys can follow behind." Scott hastily made his way to Patrick Smythe's truck and thanked him profusely and shook his hand. The Fixer and Crazy Yaz got back into the rental and followed the line of pick-up trucks to the East Toho Marina, the same marina that Patrick Smythe had his Jon boat stolen from several years ago. By the time they got to the marina, Ed Turnbull was already hogtied on the dock with his own socks stuffed in his mouth. The engines were running on his house boat, but the cavalry arrived before he could leave. Rednecks were shooting their muskets in the air and giving each other high-fives. The Fixer parked the Lincoln Town car and looked at what was going on. *Is this really going to be that easy?* the Fixer thought to himself.

Calls were made, and soon, the Mexican Union and the pirates came to the marina. Lil Bit got out of the car she was riding in and ran over to Ed Turnbull. She pulled out her taser and started shocking him in the neck. He laid there, on his stomach, with his hands and feet tied behind him and shook as the sound of *dat dat dat dat* filled the air. After ten seconds, someone finally pulled her away.

"So, you fellas have the man you were looking for. Now, why don't the two of you take him, get in that fancy car of yours, and head north. And don't come back to the town of Narcoossee, Florida ever again, or you might find a lack of southern hospitality," Patrick Smythe stated to the Fixer. He was looking him right in the eye. The *shuck-shuck* of dozens of 12-gauge shotguns echoed over the lake. "Trust me, fellas, these guns are real. Oh, Coop and his girlfriend stay with us, never to be harmed. Do we have an understanding?"

"Yes," the Fixer replied. Ed Turnbull was loaded into the trunk, and the two men got into the car and drove north, out of Narcoossee, Florida, never to return. No one noticed a white Chevy Trailblazer pulling out of the marina parking lot and following the Lincoln Town car.

"So, Coop, we wanted to say thank you for helping us rid the town of Ed Turnbull. The boys and me have been talking, and we want to make you an honorary member of Company A 6th Florida Regiment," Patrick Smythe said to Scott Cooper. He was handed a Daisy air rifle with a steak knife taped to the end and a grey uniform. "Your musket is on order. And I need the steak knife back; it's part of a set." Most of the town was at the marina at this point, and the whole crowd cheered. A blue '66 Mustang pulled into the parking lot of East Toho Marina, and Tori Lisicki quickly got out and ran to Scott. She hugged him and asked if he was ok. And he was more than ok.

After being reunited with his mother and grandmother at Blair Street station in the London Underground, the family made it back to the hotel and waited for Scott's father to come. When Charles Cooper arrived to the hotel room, he was greeted by his wife and his two sons, who rushed him at the door. They were all talking rapidly about the days adventures. One by one, they told him what had happened from their perspective. Scott left out the part about the man who stole the woman's wallet because he wanted to concentrate on the part where he was a hero. After Scott's father heard all the tales, he looked at Scott and said these words that would remain with Scott Cooper the rest of his life: "Son, I'm proud of you."

Instead of having dinner at the expensive restaurant at the hotel, Charles Cooper cancelled his reservations and took the family to Scott's favorite restaurant at the time: McDonalds. Over a dinner of Big Macs and chocolate milkshakes, the whole family would brag about Scott and the many things he would do in his life. And that would be the one and only time in his life that Scott Dow Cooper would feel like a hero. Until now.

Scott Cooper hugged his beautiful girlfriend and looked out on the residents of Narcoossee, Florida and felt like a *real* hero. Instead of just his family celebrating him, it was the whole town. He saw men and women of color coming together. The Mexican migrant workers were arm in arm with the good 'ole boys. The couple of black families that lived in the area were there also to commemorate the man whole helped rid the town of the evil Ed Turnbull. For the very first time in his life, he didn't feel insignificant or small. He didn't feel like someone sitting on the sidelines of life anymore but rather a participant. He felt like a man. A man he would be proud for his son to grow up to be.

❰ Epilogue ❱

Garret Dwayne Holstead, A.K.A. "Skeet," was released from Orange County Correctional after serving 13 months of a two-year sentence. Because he had priors in Orlando, he was transferred up there to do his time. The gate closed behind him, and he thought about what to do next. He had a cousin that could get him a job running the tilt-a-whirl at the state fair where neither sobriety nor a clean criminal record was required. He was about to make a phone call at a pay phone when a man they called Ajax on the inside appeared through the gate behind him. He was a huge, muscular man with a bald head that made him look like Mr. Clean. Skeet was about to call his cousin when a thought popped in his head, and he put the receiver back.

"Hey, Ajax! Know how to shoot pool?" he asked. Just then, a white Chevy Trailblazer pulled up, and two men got out of the back seat. They walked casually up to Skeet, and without saying a word, one struck him across the mouth with a small club, and the other quickly pulled out a burlap sack and put it over his head. They grabbed him and pushed him into the back seat of the Trailblazer and that would be the last that anyone would ever see of Garrett Dwayne Holstead.

✳

Jack Boucher sat in an uncomfortable chair at gate B37 at McCarren International Airport. He was a detective for the Las Vegas Metropolitan Police Department, and he was waiting to pick someone up. He looked over and saw a folded-up *USA Today* on the seat next to him and picked it up. He found the sports section and started reading an article about the chances of Ohio State winning the Big Ten Conference next month. *Never gonna happen, Wisconsin's D will stop their run game,* he thought to himself. An announcement was made that Southwest Airlines flight 1162 from Orlando, Florida has landed and will be at the gate soon. Jack Boucher folded up the newspaper and put it back on the seat next to him. He stood up and waited for the passengers to exit. Soon people started pouring out. Most of them were tourists, coming to gamble and take in all that the Las Vegas strip had to offer. And then he saw the person he was waiting for. A few days earlier, Jack Boucher was transferred a phone call from the main desk from a detective in some po-dunk county in Florida going on about some woman scamming a charity. *And what's this have to do with me?* Jack Boucher thought to himself. And then the detective said her name. *Jessica Driskoll.* The name caused him to sit up in his chair and take the phone cradled in his shoulder into his hand.

"What was the name again?" Jack Boucher asked the detective.

"Jessica Driskoll. I pulled her record up and saw she had priors out there and figured you wanted first crack at her. What a piece of work she is," Detective Finnell said. Jack Boucher was especially interested in Jessica Driskoll because he was the detective that arrested her for check fraud several years ago. This case was personal to him because Jessica had unknowingly used Jack Boucher's mother-in-law's stolen check book to write $2,000 in bad checks. He was there at the sentencing, and when she walked by on her way to jail, she looked at him and smiled, like it was no big deal. So, when she slowly walked off the plane and up the ramp being escorted by a U.S. Marshal, a certain satisfaction came over Detective Jack Boucher.

"She's all yours," the marshal said. "Know a good pizza place out here? I don't leave until the morning."

"Metro Pizza, hands down," Detective Jack Boucher responded without hesitation. He handcuffed her and escorted her out to the parking lot to his unmarked police car. He opened the back door and placed his hand on her head as she entered the back seat. As he started the car and backed out, Jessica Driskoll was telling him all the lewd things she would do to him if he just let her go.

"Can't we talk this over?" Jessica asked from the back seat. She winked at him in the rear-view mirror and smiled. Jack Boucher shook his head, sighed, and drove out of the parking garage to take Jessica Driskoll to jail, for the third time. She currently resides at Indian Springs State Penitentiary.

✳

Lenny Kawalski was sifting through the mail on his desk when he came across a handwritten envelope with his name on it and no return address but an Orlando postmark. He took the envelope opener and sliced through the crease. Inside were two tickets, first row, 50-yard line for the Big Ten Championship. The University of Wisconsin Badgers would host the Ohio State University Buckeyes and blow them out 44-10. Lenny Kawalski and his wife sat and enjoyed the game when an announcer recognized him as the camera panned the audience. He was identified as number 71, and at half-time, Lenny Kawalski and five other former players walked out onto the field to be commemorated. When the announcer said Lenny's name, the crowd erupted with chants of "Len-ney! Len-ney! Len-ney!" It would go down as one of the proudest moments of his life.

❋

Lucille the three-legged alligator would live to the age of 50, the normal life expectancy. One day, she climbed onto her favorite log to sun herself, fell asleep, and never woke up again. After two days, some fishermen pulled her off the log and dragged her to the boat ramp at the abandoned fish camp. It took a flatbed tow truck to pull her out of the water. She was then taken to a taxidermist, where she was stuffed and preserved. An anonymous person paid the bill and had her taken to Granted Wishes Village where she replaced Pete the Possum as the new mascot. Of course, a 13-foot alligator at the entrance to the Administration building seemed menacing, so the board decided to put over-sized sunglasses and a hat with plastic daisies on her. Marie, the receptionist with the pleasant voice, did the recording for the speaker.

❋

The clerk at the Home Depot looked at the items in the cart, thought it was suspicious, and then looked at the two men standing before her. A very tall man in a black suit wearing sunglasses and an eastern European man in Puma running sweats and a black leather jacket looked blankly at her. In the cart were: a battered powered jig saw, a box of industrial strength 25-gallon trash bags, a roll of duct tape, two sets of rubber gloves, two sets of plastic goggles, two painter's scrubs, and a bottle of Purell.

Ed Turnbull's right leg was found by a custodian at a rest area on I-4, south of Deland, Florida. It was in a trash can wrapped in a black, plastic bag. His left leg was also found wrapped in a black plastic bag in a parking lot of a biker bar in Daytona Beach. His head was found by a fisherman in Jacksonville, Florida bobbing in the water underneath a bridge. His right arm was found tightly wrapped, leaning against a drive thru speaker at a Wendy's in Brunswick, Georgia. The left arm was never found. Because the torso was found in Savannah, Georgia, the medical examiners in Florida shipped the pieces there for "re-assembly."

The Fixer was tired from the driving and needed to stretch his legs, so he pulled the Lincoln Town car into a rest area on the Jersey Turnpike. He got out and was heading to the building to get a soda when he noticed a white Chevy Trailblazer pull into the parking place next to his rental. He thought about going back because his senses started to tingle like something was wrong. But Crazy Yaz was asleep in the front seat of the car, and he shrugged it off as sleep deprivation and continued to the vending machines. When he got his soda, the Fixer walked back to his car to see a man standing in front of his car with his arms folded across his chest. He was a little shorter than the Fixer and had a rich, dark tan. The Fixer noticed a small scar just above his right eye, and his blond hair peaked out underneath the Fedora he was wearing. And he was wearing a short sleeve, button down *Salt Life* shirt, khakis, and leather sandals. The man kept his arms folded and slowly walked to the Fixer. When he was three feet away, he stopped and looked at him.

"We have a problem. Do you know who I am?" the man asked the Fixer. He shook his head but kept gazing at him. What the Fixer didn't know was the man who Crazy Yaz shot in the citrus grove was one Fredrick McCoy, younger brother of Bruce McCoy, the grandson of William "Bill" McCoy, the bootlegger. He owned several marinas and boating businesses all across the east coast of Florida, which was a cover for the smuggling operation he ran. Any illegal contraband that came into the United States from Jacksonville to Miami came through him. When his younger brother failed to check in, he drove over to his house and found it had been broken into. He went to the office and looked at the video footage of the cameras he had installed in the house. And that's how he knew Crazy Yaz kidnapped Fred at gunpoint, and later, two rednecks would come in and take an envelope. "My name is Bruce McCoy, and I am one nasty 'sum bitch. I can tell you're one nasty 'sum bitch, too. So, I'm going to talk to you man to man. I run things on the east coast of Florida. Well, let me correct myself, I run Florida. The Governor thinks he does, but I got him elected, so you get the picture. Anyways, you Russians didn't ask me permission to come do business in my state. And that's just not how southern gentlemen do business. Am I right?" He looked at the Fixer and smiled, then got solemn. "Your friend in the front seat," he jerked his thumb to the Lincoln. "He's responsible for the disappearance of my little brother. Chances are he did something stupid that warranted whatever happened to him. He definitely wasn't the brightest lure in the tackle box, but none the less, he's kin, and I can't let it go. So, here's what's going to happen," Bruce McCoy said. He unfolded his arms and put his right hand in the air. Out of the white Chevy Trailblazer, three men emerged and started walking towards them. The Fixer sized them up and knew they all had handguns in their waistband underneath their shirts. He assessed the situation before him. *I could take out the main guy and possibly one or two others, but it'll be messy, and there are innocents all around. And that leaves the other to shoot him dead.* "There will be consequences for your friends' actions, and you are to deliver a message to that greasy Russian, Nikolai Dvorchek, that Florida is not open for business." The man spoke calmly and with authority. "I must say, I liked how you disposed of Ed Turnbull. Very creative. You saved me dragging him behind a boat with chum in his pockets." The man in the hat laughed, turned around, and he and his men got into the Trailblazer and sped off. The Fixer approached his car and saw Yazoff "Crazy Yaz" Klebnikov dead in the front seat. A fishing gaff is a small pole with a large, sharp hook on the end, and it is used for pulling large fish into a boat. This particular fishing gaff was currently impaled through the right eye socket, and the tip of a blade from the filet knife stuck through his neck protruded out of his Adam's apple. *This complicates things,* the Fixer thought to himself. He took his jacket off and placed it over Crazy Yaz and walked around to the driver's side. He continued up the Jersey turnpike and made his way north. He was contracted to erase the fat business man and bring the nephew back to Nikolai. Dead or alive was a problem for the Russians to work out. He could very easily disappear and start up again in another country, but for some reason, he liked this Bruce McCoy. And there was sure to be some fallout over the death of Russian crime boss family member. *This hick might have started a gang war between the Russian mob and the Florida underground. This will definitely be interesting.*

✳

A year had passed since Scott and Julianna divorced. It was a rainy afternoon, and Carlos was at his Dad's place, so Julianna poured herself a glass of red wine and went to work cleaning out her bedroom closet. She reached for a box on the top shelf when the shoe box on top came down and hit the floor. Out poured all the love letters Scott had written to her when they were dating. There was every note he left on her car and every card he ever gave her. She sat on the floor and read every one and started to cry. *He really isn't such a bad guy. And he is the father of my only child.* The following Monday, she went to her lawyer and changed the child support and visitation to favor Scott. And on his birthday, she bought him a guitar to replace the one she burnt in the BBQ grill. It took some time, but the ice started to thaw. They wanted to be civil to one another for Carl's sake, so they started talking more and eventually came to the conclusion that they were better off as friends than they ever were as husband and wife. She started casually dating the office manager where she worked, and as time passed, she did heal. Not only was she alright with Scott dating Tori, she invited them both over for her annual Christmas party. It was a little awkward at first, but Julianna warmed up to Tori, and by the end of the evening, they were best friends and traded secrets about Scott. He walked into the kitchen where they were both drinking wine, and they abruptly stopped talking, looked at one another, and burst out laughing.

"What?" he asked.

✵

Robert Finnell remained with the Osceola County Sheriff's Department as a detective and had a decorated career. Rush was playing a five-city tour in Florida, and he had tickets to three of them. The third show was at the West Palm Beach Auditorium, and he had second row, aisle seats. They were half-way through the first set when a fan the aisle over from Robert ran to the stage and jumped up. Without thinking, Robert ran up and tackled the guy from behind before he had a chance to take a selfie with Alex Lifeson. The band didn't miss a beat and continued on with their song, "Digital Man," a personal favorite of Scott and Robert's growing up. Security rushed on stage and escorted the man off. Robert got to enjoy the rest of the show back stage and even got a "thumbs up" from Neil Peart during the drum solo. The following Monday, he tendered his resignation from the police department and took the position of head of security of the remaining Rush tour, which spanned 50 cities, 12 countries, and 4 continents. He fell in love with a back-up singer from the opening band and got married at the end of the tour. He currently lives in St. Augustine, Florida with his wife and five children and continues to tour with the band.

✵

Janeen Turnbull Noble had a disposable income, an army of attorneys, and plenty of free time on her hands, so she quickly gained control of her younger brother's assets once he was legally declared dead. He never married, nor had any children, so there wasn't much dispute in the courts. The fact that Janeen Turnbull Noble was a pillar of the community and even donated a building to Florida Atlantic University helped expedite things. She closed Gordy's Taco Shop and sold it for almost nothing to a nice family from the Philippines. And once more, the paintings on the wall were changed. Down came the pictures of burros and desert landscapes and up went paintings of panda bears and dragons. And the cactus was replaced with bamboo. Janeen Turnbull Noble had a stipulation in the contract that all the employees from the taco shop were offered a job. Jose Casidilla became their new head cook at Pandora's Chinese Emporium. Within a week, the stray cat population diminished to zero in Narcoossee, Florida. *Here we go again,* Jose thought to himself, *at least we're moving up the food chain.*

Janeen Turnbull Noble demolished the Pirate's Booty strip club and built a park with monkey bars, swings, and a big grass soccer field. Several BBQ grills and picnic tables were on the perimeter. She built a community center for child care, after-school programs, and job training. All of it paid in full without any financial drain on the community. Soon, it would be the center of the town that every event would start or finish at. Homecoming parades, fishing tournaments, and of course, the battle, as the locals would call it, all happened there. Any employees from the Pirate's Booty that decided to stay in Narcoossee were offered jobs. No one knew, but Lil Bit had a Masters degree in English Literature from Pepperdine University, and she went on to teach conversational English at the center to the migrant population. Not long after, Sophia Casidilla would offer Spanish classes, and that's how a small, southern town in the back waters of Florida became bilingual. She would always chuckle to herself to see a room full of beer drinking, bass fishing, gun shooting rednecks saying in unison, "*Hola, como esta?*" At the beginning, the white population expected everyone to speak English, but now there was a culture barrier broken, and it occurred to everyone that there are lots of languages out there in the world outside of Narcoossee, Florida. So as a manner of town pride, the Mexicans would speak in their broken English, and the rednecks would respond in their broken Spanish. It always produced a lot of laughter, and once again, brought the town together.

Janeen Turnbull Noble gave the septic pump truck to her little brother's competitor in the business, Chester's Septic Services, for free and sold him all of his contracts. She did put a clause in the paperwork about following safe and responsible disposal methods. Anything so much as a citation would bring the wraith of Mrs. Noble and the law offices of Cohen, Hyams, and Berkowitz.

On March 27th, the year after Ed Turnbull's capture, the civil war re-enactment of the Battle of Narcoossee Mill took place as it did every year. But this year was different. Any racial tensions the town had were gone. One man, as evil as he was, brought them together. Scott Cooper was there, dressed in his ill-fitting Confederate uniform and his replica musket. *I'm average height and weight, how hard can it be to get a uniform that fits!* He thought the event was silly considering the South lost, but the educator in him liked preserving history. Tori Lisicki and his son Carl sat on a blanket and cheered along with the rest of the town. There was no record of any pirates being present at the Battle of Narcoossee Mill, but Patrick Smythe made an exception this year and the years to come. If any person was shot and didn't fall down dead, Lil Bit would run out on the field and shock them with her taser. Afterwards, the whole town had a pot-luck dinner. The fried chicken and potato salad were right next to the refried beans and enchiladas. Patrick Smythe even found a mariachi band in Orlando that played Garth Brooks' covers. When the sun went down, a big bonfire was built, and everyone drank beer and told stories of their role in the demise of Ed Turnbull.

Patrick Smythe sat by the bonfire and smiled. He took a pull off of his beer and thought about everything that happened. He saw how people could come together when they needed to, if they had a common cause. And he wondered if his great-grandfather, G.B. Smythe, was looking down at him from heaven, smiling and pleased that the feud between the Turnbulls and the Smythes was finally over. He did extend an invitation to Ed Turnbull's older sister, Janeen Turnbull Noble, but she politely declined stating a prior engagement. *Maybe not all Turnbull's are bad. Just a few bad seeds in the bloodline*, he thought to himself. Patrick Smythe talked to the other citrus farmers in the area, and they agreed to work out ways to keep the workers there full time rather than leaving right after season. So, they found work for them year round, and it worked out for everyone. The workers didn't have to leave and go north to pick peaches in Georgia in the off season. And the farmers had help that felt invested in the process and not just hands .And every farmer also agreed to donate one acre of land to a migrant family, so they could own their own land and grow their own trees. Within ten years, poverty was wiped out in the town of Narcoossee, Florida.

✳

The Fixer pulled up to the cell phone store in Newark, New Jersey and drove around to the back entrance and parked. He got out and knocked three times on the back door. It opened and there stood the man with no neck. *"Da,"* he said.

"Get me Nikolai," the Fixer said. The man with no neck looked at him nervously, turned around, and disappeared into the store. A minute later, Nikolai appeared in the doorway. The Fixer wore his normal poker face, so Nikolai didn't know anything was wrong until he looked over the Fixer's shoulders and saw a figure in the front seat with a jacket over his head. Nikolai looked back at the Fixer. "What happened? I didn't think I needed to specify I wanted my nephew back, ALIVE!"

"There was a problem," the Fixer replied. "Apparently your nephew made a man disappear that was related to someone pretty important. I mean, really important. That was out of my hands, but I did bring you your nephew. So out of good faith, you can keep the other half of my fee, and we've concluded business."

"OUT OF GOOD FAITH! CONCLUDED BUSINESS!" Nikolai reached for his .45 that was holstered underneath his arm when the Fixer chopped him in the throat so fast, he never saw it coming. Before he could bring his hand up to his neck, the Fixer thrusted the palm of his right hand into Nikolai's nose causing it to shatter. He slowly fell backwards dead onto the floor and landed with a loud *thud*. The Fixer grabbed the gun and sought out the man with no neck and he found him at the counter. He was on the phone when he saw the Fixer pointing a gun at him. He slowly put the phone down and quickly raised his hands up. The Fixer cocked the hammer.

"Are we cool?"

"*Da,*" the man with no neck replied nervously.

"Good. Who were you on the phone with? New York?"

"*Da,*"

"Good. If I were you, I'd disappear to the mid-west, find a nice girl, and settle down. Open a Russian deli that specializes in borscht or something. I don't know, but I would advise you to remove yourself from this situation. Yesterday." The Fixer hit him on the head with the butt of the gun, and he collapsed unconscious. He walked out the back of the cell phone store and was headed to his car when he stopped, turned around, and went back inside. He bent down and leaned over Nikolai Dvorchek.

"Oh, I almost forgot. Bruce McCoy says you can't do business in Florida anymore." He got up and went to the rental and grabbed his small bag. It was chilly, so he grabbed the jacket off of Crazy Yaz and put it on. There was going to be a shit storm over what just happened, so the Fixer decided to vanish. He hailed a cab and went back to his apartment. He packed up what few things he had and headed to the airport. He was going to escape to a destination known as a sanctuary for people on the run. When he got to the counter, he handed the man a fake driver's license and a credit card with the same name.

"And where are we headed tonight, Mr. Stefano?" the man behind the counter asked.

"Las Vegas, Nevada. One way."

✳

Bruce McCoy and his crew drove south on I-95, and when they crossed the Florida/Georgia state-line, Bruce McCoy got a phone call. He hated being out of his state, so he immediately felt better once they crossed.

"Talk to me, my boy," he said into the cell phone. After listening to the voice on the other end of the phone, he asked, "He did what?" Bruce McCoy listened to the exploits of the man he encountered at the rest stop, which after an exhaustive search revealed only his alias, the Fixer. "Ok, so after he took out Nikolai, what did he do next?...went to the airport?...where was he going?...Vegas?...you did good. Return back to the Homestead, and we'll figure out what to do." Bruce McCoy put the phone back into his pocket, stared at the lights of Jacksonville, and thought about the Fixer and what he had done. *I really like this guy. I could use a man like that on my crew. I'll contact my cousin on the west coast to find him and make him an offer. He won't be hard to find.* As the white Chevy Trailblazer traveled south to the Homestead in Jupiter, Florida, Bruce McCoy contemplated his immediate future, which at some point would include the Russian mob. If he kept things on his turf, he could win, but this "Fixer" forced his hand. *We'll just have to move the time frame up.*

❋

King Leopold got Tori Lisicki a small part in *The Music Man* at Hal Abrams' Dinner Club and Theater. There, seated in the crowd, was a Disney executive appeasing his elderly parents. When he saw her, he immediately gave Hal his business card and told him to give it to the young lady. A week later, she was the new Snow White at Walt Disney World.

Tori and Scott continued to date, and their love for one another grew. When he moved up to Orlando, she moved in with him. Because she loved the children there, she continued to play the part of Princess Tori at Granted Wishes Village, though on a limited, volunteer status. One night, Scott had planned a date and drove the two of them all the way down to Narcoossee. They had dinner at Hubba's Grub and Subs, and he was recognized by a patron there and received a free slice of apple pie. He then took her to Granted Wishes Village. Henry Weisel was at the gate, and he saluted as they drove passed. He took her to the dock, and they sat there and listened to the crickets. There was a half-moon that shined overhead and there was a light, cool breeze blowing off the lake. Scott Cooper reached into his pocket and pulled something out. He got down on one knee and opened the tiny box containing a diamond ring.

"Tori, will you marry me? Can I be your Prince Charming?" he asked. He had butterflies in his stomach, and he tried to keep his hands steady. Tori brought her hands up to her mouth, and a tear fell from her left eye, down her cheek. "And if you say 'ding ding ding, we have a winner,' we're getting married in Vegas by Elvis." She started to laugh and picked him up. She hugged and kissed him repeatedly.

"You've always been my Prince Charming! Yes! Yes! Yes!" she shouted. They made out under the moonlight in the very spot where Scott Cooper decided to change his life two years prior.

✹

After he got let go from Granted Wishes Village, Scott Cooper decided to end his short-lived career in law enforcement. Tori got her brother to help get him a job waiting tables at the Tommy Bahama's at Pointe Orlando. After paying for the football tickets, getting Lucille stuffed, and Tori's ring, he had enough money left over to purchase a computer built within the last decade and a functioning printer. He was going to pursue his dream of writing a book. He now had the subject matter. He did some research and found out there were authors named Scott Cooper and S. Cooper, so he was going to need a pen name. One of his favorite song writers growing up was Chris Moore, and Scott's middle name was

Dow, so he decided to play around with that. All he needed was a title. As he sat there, looking at a blank computer screen, it hit him and he started typing.

Wish

by C. Dow Moore

✳